Praise for *Jesse's Girl*

"A fun, sexy, suck-me-in read."

—Katie McGarry, author of *Nowhere But Here*

"Highly enjoyable."

—*Kirkus Reviews*

"Kenneally branches out with this book while keeping all the elements readers have come to love about her books: friendship, family life, romance, strong female characters, and a glimpse at past characters... *Jesse's Girl* is the perfect summer novel hitting all the right notes."

—*VOYA*

Praise for *Breathe, Annie, Breathe*

★ "In this expertly paced and realistic romance, Kenneally gives Annie's sorrow a palpable weight, but she writes with such ease that Annie and her goals become exceedingly likable and familiar and never overwrought."

—*Booklist*, Starred Review

"*Breathe, Annie, Breathe* is an emotional, heartfelt, and beautiful story about finding yourself after loss and learning to love. Her best book yet."

—Jennifer L. Armentrout, *New York Times* bestselling author of *Wait for You*

Praise for *Things I Can't Forget*

"Kenneally's books have quickly become must-reads."

—*VOYA*

"Entertaining and poignant."

—*School Library Journal*

"[A] compassionate and nuanced exploration of friendship, love, and maturing religious understanding."

—*Publishers Weekly*

Also by Miranda Kenneally

Coming Up for Air

Coming Up for Air

MIRANDA KENNEALLY

sourcebooks
fire

Published by Sourcebooks Fire, an imprint of Sourcebooks, Inc.
P.O. Box 4410, Naperville, Illinois 60567-4410
(630) 961-3900
Fax: (630) 961-2168
www.sourcebooks.com

Library of Congress Cataloging-in-Publication Data is on file with the publisher.

Printed and bound in the United States of America.
VP 10 9 8 7 6 5 4 3 2 1

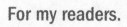
For my readers.

A Day in the Life

Wake up at 4:15 a.m.

Swim

Eat breakfast

Shower

Second breakfast

School

Snack between classes

Lunch

More class

Swim

Swim

Swim some more

Snack

Eat dinner

Homework

Sleep

Dream about swimming (and eating)

When I'm not in the pool, I'm counting the minutes until I can dive back in, so most of the time my bushy, light-brown hair is wet and reeks of chlorine.

This is the story of my life.

But Friday nights are different because my friends and I have a tradition. We always meet for dinner at Jiffy Burger to talk about our lives. (Okay, mostly our love lives.)

My little group has been doing this since we were thirteen, when we still had to ride our bikes or bum rides from our moms. We understand each other. My best friend Levi and I spend all our time in the pool, while Hunter is the baseball team's star pitcher, and Georgia's a gymnast-turned-cheerleader. Without a lot of time for anything but school and practice, we always carve out time for our Friday night dinners, and tonight is no different.

Hunter has barely said a word since I sat down. His eyes keep darting around Jiffy Burger and out the window, where a light January snow is steadily falling. He doesn't even say thank you when the waitress delivers our usual salads, fries, tater tots, and shakes.

"What's wrong with you?" I ask.

Levi starts laughing so hard he snorts. Georgia is giggling too.

I pop one of Levi's fries in my mouth and he steals one of my tater tots. "What's going on?" I ask through a mouthful.

"Mr. Goodwin caught Hunt in Shelby's room last night," Georgia says.

"Shit," I say.

With a red face, Hunter rips into his burger and chews. His eyes sweep the restaurant again.

"He's terrified Mr. Goodwin is gonna show up here and pulverize him," Levi says.

"Back up," I say. "I need details."

Hunter is chewing slowly, probably so he doesn't have to answer.

Levi jumps in. "You know how the Goodwin manor has all those secret passageways from the Civil War? Hunt's been sneaking into Shelby's room over the past few weeks."

"I had no idea you guys were so serious," I say, spearing lettuce with my fork.

"We're not," Hunter grumbles. "We're still just fooling around." He stuffs a fry in his mouth.

"Does she know that?" Georgia asks.

"It was her idea!" Hunter says. "You know I want to go out with her."

Swimming takes up all my time, so I've never dated anyone, or really made out with a guy for that matter. Hunter has someone to make out with on a regular basis now, and I'm pretty jealous. I will have to live vicariously through him.

"Hunter," I say. "Story. Now."

"I was making out with Shelby in her room—"

"Without your shirt on," Levi cuts in.

"Without my shirt on, when her dad burst in. He chased me down the stairs and out the front door."

I lean back in the booth. "Shit," I say again.

"So I get this call at two in the morning," Levi says. "It was Hunt calling to ask me to pick him up from the Exxon station."

Hunter slumps. "I left my keys and phone in Shelby's room."

"And your shirt." Levi flashes me a grin. "Did I mention that when I picked him up he was shirtless? He ran shirtless through the snow!"

"I left that in her room too," Hunter mutters.

"At least you had your pants," I say encouragingly.

"I'm glad her dad didn't have a gun," Hunter says.

"So you rescued Hunter. This is why you were so wrecked at practice," I say to Levi, who was incredibly sluggish in the pool this morning. He nods and shrugs. I'm not hurt Levi didn't say something to me—he's never talkative in the morning because he's not a morning person.

"So now what happens?" Georgia interrupts. "Are you still gonna see Shelby?"

Hunter plays with his fries. "I hope so."

"You must really like her," I say.

"You'd probably be risking death to go back to her house," Levi says.

"Then it's a good thing it has all those secret passageways," Hunter says, and we all burst out laughing.

This is what it's always like for us. As far as I know, we've never kept any secrets from each other, and I don't know what I'll do without them when we leave for college this fall. Georgia to the University of Tennessee. Hunter to the Air Force Academy, where he'll train to be an officer and play baseball. Levi to University of Texas, and me to Cal-Berkley, two of the best swimming schools.

The four of us started hanging out in seventh grade because we had special schedules at school. Levi and I needed to leave before last period for club practice in Nashville. Georgia left early too. At the time, she was a serious competitive gymnast and trained with a professional coach every day. And because our school didn't have one, Hunter went across town for last period to attend a junior ROTC program that his grandfather wanted him in. This meant our school didn't require any of us to take gym class, which messed up our schedules, which meant we had to eat lunch with the sixth graders. None of us would be caught dead sitting with a sixth grader, so we started hanging out and never really stopped.

Still famished after my run this afternoon, I take a big bite of salad followed by a tater tot. Levi is on to his second cheeseburger. He and I swim six or seven times a week, three hours a day, and when we're not swimming, Coach has us lifting weights or doing cardio. We're *always* hungry. Georgia watches Levi chewing. That's when I notice she's only been picking at her fries, and her shake is untouched.

"You okay?" I ask her.

"I got an email from an assistant coach at Tennessee," Georgia says. She'll be on the cheerleading squad starting this fall.

5

"I'm still shocked they want you on the team," Hunter says, sipping his iced tea through a straw. "There's nothing a Tennessee fan hates more than Georgia."

"That's not true," Levi says. "They hate Alabama more."

Georgia smirks. "I don't think Tennessee fans will give a crap what my name is once they see me do a roundoff back handspring back tuck."

"What did the coach say?" I ask, to get us back on topic. Our tangents are legendary.

"That I need to follow a strict diet." Georgia pops a french fry in her mouth and chews. "Like, I have to eat a certain amount of calories per day and have to count grams of carbs and fat. I can't eat cheese anymore!"

I gasp. Levi and Hunter pause in their chewing. Georgia lives for cheese. It's her favorite food and general reason for being.

"You don't need to lose weight," Hunter says. "You look great."

Georgia gives in and slurps her milkshake. "This is why I run every day. So I can eat cheese."

"I run every day so I can outrun Mr. Goodwin," Hunter replies, and the rest of us laugh.

What a sucker. I'd never get myself in a position like that.

Rather than risk another run-in with Mr. Goodwin, Hunter asked Shelby over to his house tonight, and Georgia's mom wants her home early because she has a cheerleading competition tomorrow morning in Chattanooga. So it's just me and Levi.

"Want to come back to my place?" he asks.

"Yeah, but I can't stay too late."

Tomorrow morning I'm flying to California to spend the night at Cal-Berkeley, where I'll be going to school this fall. I will be attending a special orientation for new student athletes.

In his truck on the way to his house, we play our usual game where we pretend we're on a boat with three people. We have to choose who we'd: spend one hot night with; spend an entire year sailing around the world with; throw overboard.

Levi says, "Justin Bieber, Oprah, and Donald Trump."

"That's an easy one," I reply, ticking them off on my fingers. "I'd throw Donald Trump overboard, because *obviously*. I'd have one hot night with Bieber and spend a year with Oprah. She's rich and has beach houses we could stay at when we're sailing around the Caribbean."

"You wouldn't spend a year with Bieber? He's rich and probably has nice houses."

"He's cute, but I don't think I could handle his personality. I heard he was doing yoga on top of the Empire State Building the other day."

He laughs. "Well, you gotta do your yoga somewhere, right? Okay, my turn."

"Tom Brady, Prince Harry, and Elvis."

Levi groans. He hates it when I don't give him any girls to consider. Tapping his fingers on the steering wheel, he considers his options. "I'd spend one hot night with Tom Brady—maybe some of his good luck from winning all those Super Bowls would rub off on me. I'd spend a year with Prince Harry because he's adventurous. He could get us into any party, and girls would be all over us. I'd throw Elvis overboard because he's already dead."

"You have to assume he's alive! That's against the rules."

Levi smiles at me from the driver's seat. "There are no rules in this game. Now, it's your turn. Professor Dumbledore, Marie Antoinette, and Michelle Obama."

"Ugggh."

The house is dark when we arrive, with only the porch light lit. His mom is working late, like every night. She's an executive at Rêve Records, the country music label. Ms. Lucassen says music never sleeps, and as a result, neither does she. She adores all things country—horses, rodeos, line dancing. Levi even got his name from her favorite brand of jeans.

It's after eight o'clock, and *Wheel of Fortune* is over, so Oma and Opa are already in bed. His grandparents have lived with him since he was a toddler, when his dad left his mom and moved to Texas. They're Dutch, and forbade Levi from calling them Gram and Gramps. That's what I call both sets of my grandparents. There's Ohio Gram and Gramps and Tennessee Gram and Gramps. Levi thinks it's hilarious I call them that.

Levi unlocks the front door, and his dog, Pepper, bounds up and, as usual, sticks her face in his crotch. She's a bearded collie whose gray-and-white hair always falls in her eyes like a boy in a boy band.

He scratches her floppy ears. "Hey, baby girl."

Levi flicks on a few switches to light the way to his room. When we get there, I kick off my boots and flop down on his soft bed, loving the way it bounces. He pulls his hooded gray sweatshirt off over his head, his T-shirt riding up a little to reveal ripped abs thanks to the three hundred crunches a day that Coach orders.

I love that sweatshirt. His last name is embroidered on the breast in cursive: *Lucassen*. Soft from so many washings, it smells like him, and I love stealing it to wear, but he always nabs it right back because it's his favorite.

He places his wallet on top of his desk next to stacks of books and dozens of trophies. He lies down next to me, looking comfy in a pair of running tights with long athletic shorts over them. Even though Ms. Lucassen pressures him to wear jeans and nice button-downs, I never see him in anything but Speedos, athletic clothes, and the silver chain his mom gave him. It has a little pendant that says *Make Waves*.

I grab his iPad from the messy nightstand, which is covered by empty Gatorade bottles and a stack of Harry Potter paperbacks, and turn on some music. Levi starts fiddling with his phone.

"You better not be playing Candy Crush again," I say. Coach

Josh nearly took his phone away this morning because he was tapping the screen instead of diving in the pool.

"I'm texting Molly."

"Who?"

"The girl I met in Clarksville a couple weeks ago."

Levi always finds a way to sneak out at meets to hook up, especially when we're in hotels and Coach can't keep an eye on him every waking minute. He's only seventeen, but could pass for a college guy. At six foot five and 190 pounds, he's a beast. I look tiny beside him, and I'm five foot ten. Girls love his body, with his long, lean, muscled torso, and sleek blond hair. He says sex helps him take the edge off. I don't care how he chooses to spend his free time, but a random hook-up at a meet has always made me nervous.

Not only would it distract me, it could hurt my reputation. I can't risk other athletes thinking I get around. *Especially Roxy*. My rival already gets in my head in the pool. I can't give her anything to lord over me.

But believe me, I really want to make out with somebody. The last—and only—person I've kissed is Hunter during an ill-advised game of truth or dare two years ago, when we each declared the other the worst kisser ever. *Maybe I need to play truth or dare more often*, I muse.

Levi's phone keeps buzzing as he types.

"Are you sexting?" I tease.

"No," he says a little too quickly, totally guilty, and then he cracks up. "I don't know actually. Do you think her telling me 'I need to kiss your plump lips ASAP' is sexting?"

"Plump lips? Did she really say that?" I try to look over his shoulder at his phone, but he elbows me away. "What did you say back?"

"That I want to touch her bazongas."

I bury my face in his pillow. "Nooo. You did not."

He's still laughing. "Okay, fine. I told her I finally cleared level 181 of Candy Crush."

"How romantic."

"She responded that her 'lips have been known to taste like candy.'" He cocks his head, thinking. "I'd agree with that."

I roll my eyes. "Are you into her?"

He stares at his phone, thumbs tapping the screen. "She's nice…but I don't want anything serious."

What he means is, even if he did want a relationship, he'd have no time for it. Next week is conferences, two weeks later is regionals, and two weeks after that is the high school state championship. Then, if we qualify—which I will totally die if we *don't* qualify—we have Junior Nationals in Huntsville with our club team, New Wave. Then there are two important long-course meets, leading all the way up to the Olympic trials in June. I eat, sleep, and breathe the trials. It's on my mind every waking minute, and I haven't even qualified for them yet.

We. Are. Busy.

Friday nights are literally our only downtime because we don't swim doubles or lift weights on Fridays. This is why we don't have time for serious dating: every other day of the week, we'd be asleep by now after a hard workout.

Speaking of which, I'm exhausted, and my muscles are tight. I stretch my arms above my head.

"Your shoulder still bothering you?" he asks. I nod, and he motions for me to flip onto my stomach so he can work on this knot from Hades that won't go away.

His strong hands massage my shoulder until the dog jumps on the bed to interrupt my bliss. Pepper presses her paws on my back and barks.

"Pepper! That's my job," Levi says, motioning for her to get off the bed. He turns to me. "So. You excited for tomorrow?"

I hesitate. Based on my swimming record, Cal offered me a scholarship last year. I can't wait to kick some ass swimming in college, but I dread the idea of moving away from my friends. Especially Levi. We've never been apart for more than a week.

"I'm sort of excited...? I don't know."

Levi nudges me. "You'll have fun this weekend. I had a great time visiting Texas. Some guys from the team took me out to dinner and then we went to a party. Do you think you'll do something like that?"

"I'm not sure... I wish we were going to the same college. I don't want to leave you."

I look back over my shoulder at him, and he gives me a supportive but sad smile.

My friend doesn't want to leave me either.

Rival

I feel like I suddenly disappeared from America and turned up in Italy.

That is my first impression of Cal-Berkeley. The white clock tower looks like something you'd see in Florence. I wouldn't be surprised to come across a naked David statue. Though the campus could be covered in naked statues, and I wouldn't care, because it's the best swimming school in the country. I've worked my ass off to be here and now that I am? I'm bouncing on my toes with excitement.

My flight took off at the crack of dawn. Even though I'm used to waking up early for practice, I feel a little off. I've traveled without my parents before but never this far and not without Coach Josh. It would have been nice if Mom and Dad could have come with me, but as event planners, Saturdays and Sundays are their busiest days of the week. The trip so far has gone fine; I made it to California in one piece and took a cab from the airport. The biggest problem I've encountered is sitting in coach on the plane. Having such long legs is great for swimming, but not for traveling.

Using the campus map on my phone, I navigate to a board-room in Haas Pavilion. This is where I'll be meeting up with other new student athletes for a tour, and later on I'll spend the night with a student host in her dorm.

I walk into the boardroom and gasp when I see the black hair with purple and pink streaks, and the diamond nose stud.

Roxy is here.

Shit.

She looks over at me, her mouth falling open a little, but she shuts it quickly and resumes her conversation with a man wear-ing a yellow Cal polo, pretending as if she doesn't know me. She knows exactly who I am.

I'm her former best friend.

I met Roxy six years ago when we were eleven. After doing our laps at the Sportsplex, Levi and I would spend our summer days at Normandy Lake behind his house. We loved play-ing cards on the beach and doing tricks off the diving board attached to the floating wooden barge. That's where I first saw Roxy, swimming along the rope line separating the shallow water from the deep. Her swift, graceful movements reminded me of a dolphin.

Later I cornered her by the snack stand over on the public beach. "Who do you swim for?"

"Huh?"

"Are you on a team? Tullahoma, maybe?"

She shook her head, unwrapping her ice cream sandwich. "I asked my parents a few years ago, but they said no. It's too expensive, and they don't want to get up early to drive me to practices."

"You should be swimming. You're great."

I told Coach Josh about her, and as soon as he saw her raw talent, he worked with New Wave to get her a club team scholarship. Even then he could tell she'd be unstoppable.

Since her parents were wedded to sleeping in, my mom and Levi's agreed to let her carpool with us, and for two years, the three of us were inseparable. I loved Levi, of course, but it was nice having a girl around. Especially when I got my period and had to figure out how to use tampons so I would never miss a practice. We even shared tips on how best to shave our legs.

But then the tension started. When I'd get faster in the pool, she'd work hard to beat me, and then I'd work harder to beat her. It started pissing us both off, but I figured friendship came before winning. She didn't feel the same. She's too competitive. Roxy resented that even though she had natural talent, I was faster in the pool. But it wasn't like I winged it. I had to work hard.

Then one day Coach Josh took me aside to say the Memphis Marines club swim team had recruited Roxy away from us. Her family, who by then understood Roxy was going places, agreed to move three hours away to Memphis. I cried when she left.

At first we kept in touch, texting every day, but the special treatment from the Marines made her snobby. My texts went unanswered. When I saw her at meets, she either laughed at my team or ignored me.

Every time she'd beat one of my times, she'd brag about it online. Once, after I lost a race to her, she took a picture of me with a horrible look on my face and posted it with the caption: *Second Place.*

When I bowed out of the Speedo Grand Classic because I'd strained a hamstring, Roxy posted on Twitter: *"Maggie King knew she wouldn't be able to win. That's why she pulled out. She's scared!"*

The next time I lost to her, she posted yet another unattractive picture with the tag: *Runner Up.*

Those pictures and their captions are on the Internet forever. She deleted them from her accounts so it doesn't look like she started them, but they're still out there. When I win races, I celebrate with my friends and hang my medals in my bedroom. I would never gloat.

Roxy's betrayal made me rage, and that's when Levi took my phone and unfriended and blocked her so I wouldn't see that crap anymore.

She did a number on me. I didn't have many friends because of my practice schedule, and after that I was pretty wary of new people, especially other girls in my swim club.

I didn't blame Roxy for moving on to a team she thought would be a better fit for her, but I felt betrayed. I'd put myself out there for her. If it weren't for me, she wouldn't have gotten the training to become one of the best swimmers in Tennessee. Not to mention, she has about ten thousand more Twitter followers than I do and people love her Instagram account. Some of her pictures get hundreds of likes.

And now? When we race against each other, she usually out-swims me, even though I'm better at backstroke than she is. I know I am. My times kill hers. But it doesn't matter how fast you are if your mind isn't in the right place. Whenever I compete against Roxy, she gets in my head, and I can't get her out. Of all the strokes, 200 backstroke is my best chance of getting an Olympic trials cut. Unfortunately, it's her best event too.

It would've been nice to have had some warning Roxy would be here, but I haven't been friends with her on Facebook or Twitter in a while. I will admit I spy from time to time, but I haven't in a few months.

I text Levi to tell him what's up, that Roxy's here, that I don't want to go to college with her, that I'm terrified she'll spaz me out at our meets this spring and I won't qualify to compete at the Olympic trials. I really, really don't want to go to Cal with her.

He replies: Enough. You're better than her. When you get home, we'll figure this out. Got it?

I type, Got it.

Levi already has an Olympic trial cut in 200 breaststroke—he got it last summer at a meet in Jacksonville. In June, he will com-pete for a spot on the US Olympic team. Only about a hundred people in the entire country will qualify in each stroke, so it's amazing Levi's got a spot in 200 breast. He's hoping to qualify for the trials in 100 breast and freestyle too.

Me? I don't have cuts in any stroke yet.

Going to the Olympics has been a dream for a long time. When I was eight years old, an elite swimmer named Allison Schmitt spoke to my club team about her career. She was still in high school but had hopes of making the next Olympic team—and then she did. I remember watching her on TV that summer, thinking, *wow, I met her*. And *wow, I want to do that too*. To walk out onto the pool deck in front of cheering fans and the entire world, and swim my heart out to win. Because I love winning.

Since I haven't qualified for the trials yet, I don't have any illusions I'll make this year's Olympic team, but Allison didn't win gold at her first Olympics. All her training built and built over the years, and it paid off when she won at her second Olympics. That's what my goal is: to train and train until I win the biggest race there is.

And Cal-Berkeley is the next step on the path to winning.

I slip my phone in the back pocket of my jeans, then make my way over to Roxy. "Hi," I tell her, and when she doesn't respond or make any effort to introduce me to the man she's talking to, I thrust a hand toward him. "I'm Maggie King."

His face lights up. "I'm Alan Watts, the athletic director. Maggie, I can't tell you how thrilled we are you chose Cal."

19

"Thank you, sir."

"Coach Pierson mentioned the swim team has a meet in Michigan this weekend, right?"

"Yeah, we couldn't find a weekend where our meets didn't clash, so I decided to skip it to come to this orientation."

"That's why Roxy is here this weekend too. I imagine you swim in many of the same meets."

"Yeah," we say simultaneously, side-eyeing each other.

When the athletic director turns away for a sec, Roxy gets in a jab: "Yep, we swim in many of the same meets...which I always win."

"In your dreams," I reply under my breath.

Before we join the academic tour with the other athletes—mostly field hockey, lacrosse, and basketball players—Roxy and I go with Mr. Watts to check out the brand-new, open-air aquatics center.

I love it. It's bright, airy, and yellow and blue Bears flags are draped over the calm blue pool. The air smells fresh and only a tiny bit chemical-y. My pool back home is humid because it's indoor. I can totally see myself swimming here in college.

The first time I ever jumped in a pool, I was two years old at a church barbeque. The way Dad tells the story, I was a crazy ass toddler my parents couldn't control. I saw the pool, took off running, and did a belly flop into the water. People started freaking out, screaming that I was going to drown, and Dad jumped in to rescue me, but by then I was doggy paddling. The way he tells the story, I was even making a pouty fish face, pretending I was a goldfish.

To this day, anytime I see water, it's hard for me to resist the pull to dive on in. The Cal pool is beautiful.

"Maybe we'll have time to grab a swim before we fly home," I tell Roxy, bouncing on my toes.

She doesn't respond.

"Are you really going to do this?" I ask.

"Do what?"

"Pretend like I don't exist."

She rolls her eyes.

That's that, I guess. What else is new?

After we spend time exploring the pool and facilities, Roxy and I join up with a group of about twenty new athletes from across the country for a campus tour of the library, dining hall, and classrooms. She immediately starts clinging to this super cute lacrosse player.

To be honest, I don't know the rules of lacrosse. It's too bad I couldn't attend the orientation for swimmers, which is next week, but I'm competing at conferences, and unless I qualify there, I can't go to regionals. Still, I don't mind checking out some of the guys. A super cute one with glasses and cropped black hair glances at me and smiles. But he's much shorter than I am. Ugh, I hate being taller than most guys.

With her arm looped around Lacrosse Boy's elbow, Roxy

stares over at me and smirks, as if to say, *I'm hotter than you, and I know it.*

I ignore her and try to focus on the tour, but she keeps laughing loudly to show off.

Is it too late to pick a new college?

The guide leads us back to Haas Pavilion, the arena where the basketball team plays, to watch their game against Stanford. The stands are already filled with rowdy fans. The guys on my tour start horsing around. Two of them rush out onto the court and pretend to shoot an imaginary basketball.

"Get off the floor!" the guide screeches, and they hurry back to the sidelines, where they keep pretending to take shots.

I don't blame them for being excited. The arena's smaller than I imagine it looks on TV, but it's still gorgeous. I take a picture of the basketball hoop and the gleaming wood floors with *Cal* written in blue.

I text the photo to Levi: Guess where I am?

Levi: Stop trying to make me jealous you evil woman

I grin at his response.

During the game I keep texting him, giving him a play-by-play. Levi wants to know what it smells like (sweat), if the seats are soft (hard), and what the fries taste like (they've got nothing on Jiffy Burger's, but I tell him they are a perfect ten just to make him jealous).

The game is great. The team beats Stanford in overtime, and

afterward, the guide leads us back to the boardroom to hear the university's president give a short speech about how thankful they are "athletes of our caliber are attending Berkeley." Then he announces that our student hosts will show us where we'll be staying tonight.

I lift my overnight bag and walk to the K—N table and tell them my name is Maggie King.

The name checker drags a finger down her list. "You're paired with Sylvia."

Please don't let her be a raging lunatic. Please don't let her be a raging lunatic.

The athletic director comes over when he hears my name, and checks a chart. "Sylvia's one of our highly talented freshmen on the dance team. She'll walk you around and you'll stay with her in MacDonald, the dorm you'll be living in this fall. All of our athletes live there freshman year."

A dance team member? That's good news. Georgia's a cheerleader, so I know all about routines. She's tried to teach me some, and I can do Beyoncé's "Single Ladies" dance. I may look like a bumbling octopus with my huge hands and flipper feet, but hey, I can do it.

I glance over at Roxy. She's animatedly talking to her host.

The AD introduces me to Sylvia, a small girl still wearing a skirt and tiny top from dancing at the basketball game earlier. She cranes her neck back to look up at me. "God, you're tall!"

"Will that be a problem?" the AD asks in a depreciating tone.

Sylvia shoots him a look and places a hand on her hip. "C'mon, Maggie. We have to go get ready."

"Ready for what?" the AD and I ask simultaneously.

"Uh, dinner in the dining hall. And a night tour of the library." Sylvia grabs my heavy overnight bag, throws it over her shoulder with surprising ease, and yanks me out of the boardroom. "I thought we'd never escape. The AD thinks the dance team is made up of idiots."

"One of my best friends is a cheerleader, and she is definitely not an idiot."

Sylvia smiles. "I like you."

She stops to put on a hoodie over her dance uniform before leading me back to her dorm, pointing out places like the Terrace Café and the bookstore along the way. The quad features a few marble statues surrounded by trees. I could definitely see myself studying there this fall.

It's Saturday night, but campus is busy and bustling. Some people are running around screaming, celebrating the basketball team's win. A group of guys wearing Greek fraternity letters—I'm not sure what they say—come spilling out of the dorms.

"Let's streak!" one hollers.

"Yes!" another replies, pumping his fist in the air. "But first let's get pizza."

I crack up. No matter where you go, guys are still guys, and that means food comes first.

"Don't eat before you streak!" I call out. "You might get cramps."

The boys laugh at my joke, then hustle down the sidewalk, presumably in search of pizza.

Watching these people goof around, I can't remember the last time I let loose. I guess when I went to a bonfire last summer with my friends and stayed out past midnight. It was fun, but you know what's even more enjoyable? Winning. Which means practice comes first. Which means I need rest in order to get up at the crack of dawn and swim my best.

Sylvia swipes her ID card in a door reader and we go inside her dorm. Two students manning the front desk greet Sylvia by name, then look back down at an iPad they're sharing. They must be watching videos while they work. I've never had time for a job, but I like the idea of greeting people as they come home.

Sylvia leads me to the stairs. "I'm on the fourth floor. You okay to walk?"

"Sure."

"Good. It doesn't matter if you live up on the eighth floor. People will give you shit if you take the elevator in MacDonald."

We hustle up to her floor and she leads me to a door with a little white board for messages. I make a mental note to remember to buy one of those, along with some markers. Inside her room, there's enough space for two beds, desks, and dressers. Pictures of dancers and cheerleaders cover the walls. A collection of medals hangs from a peg above her desk. Maybe I'll do that with my medals next year. And I could hang a bulletin board with pictures of my friends.

It's very clean in here. Much cleaner than my room. I tend to toss my dirty clothes on the floor instead of in the hamper, which drives my mom batty. Levi too. He generally invites me to his place because my room is always a pigsty. Having a roommate for the first time in my life will be different. I'll need to keep my space tidy. Wait. What if she's even messier than me? Hopefully I'll get somebody I'm compatible with. If I'm rooming with another athlete, odds are we'll be at practice most of the time, when we're not in class or sleeping.

"I hope you don't mind an air mattress."

"Not at all," I reply, taking off my jacket. "Thanks for hosting me. I bet it's weird having a swimmer instead of a dancer."

She shrugs. "We'll still have fun. What did you bring to wear?"

I look down at my ripped jeans and long-sleeved tee. "Stuff like this."

"There's a party at the basketball house. They're celebrating. We need to look cute."

I bite my bottom lip. It's not like I'm a prude. It's just, I've never been to a party-party before. I always have to wake up early on weekends, so staying out late is a no-go. What if Sylvia ditches me and I have no one to talk to? What if they only have booze to drink?

I *have* had a drink before. One time when Levi's mom was

out of town, we experimented with her liquor cabinet. Not only did it feel terrible, Coach Josh totally caught us. The next day he knew something was up when we were sluggish. I haven't had any interest in drinking since.

"I didn't bring anything to wear to a party."

She scans my body. "My neighbor plays basketball. She's about your size. We can raid her closet!"

I grin, glad this is going okay so far. Sylvia tells me to wear comfortable shoes because we'll be walking off campus to the basketball house. My black boots and distressed jeans don't look all that bad with the sparkly silver top I borrowed from her neighbor. Normally I don't dress so sexy. I'm showing a lot of skin.

Sylvia eyes me up and down. "You look hot."

"Are you sure?"

"You have a killer body. You won't be able to keep the guys away at the party."

Really? Just because I'm wearing a slinky top instead of my usual sweats and T-shirts? I mean, I'm still me, and attracting guys has never been my forte.

I text Levi a selfie to see what he thinks of my outfit.

Levi: You look really pretty, M.

Me: ☺

He sends back a picture of himself. Levi: What do you think of my outfit?

He's resting at home tonight since he swam doubles today, and looks relaxed in that gray New Wave sweatshirt I want so bad.

Me: You're red carpet ready!

Levi: Have a good time tonight.

I ask Sylvia, "So do all the basketball players live in this house?"

"Some of them. It's kind of a cesspit, to be honest."

"But we're going to a party there?"

"Well, *yeah*. The basketball team will be there. And I'm hoping this guy Sean from the football team comes. We made out last weekend."

"Oh."

Sylvia's only a year older, but it seems like she's a lot more mature than me. Even though I'm technically almost an adult, I feel like I haven't had any truly adult experiences. Except for, like, getting my own debit card and flying on a plane here by myself. To be honest, I haven't had many life experiences at all. I'm seventeen. I've never had a boyfriend. I certainly haven't been in any sort of situation where I needed to escape without my shirt on like Hunter did.

"Are you dating anybody?" Sylvia asks.

I avoid her eyes. "Not right now."

I'm too embarrassed to admit that other than Hunter's horrid kiss during truth or dare, I've never done anything with a guy. Much less date one. This isn't the first time I've felt behind experience-wise: Levi, Hunter, and Georgia have all had sex. Meanwhile, I'm Snow White.

She squeezes my arm. "You're gonna meet lots of guys tonight. And you won't have to feel guilty about flirting with any of them. Once you get to college, most people don't have relationships."

"What? They don't?"

"No. They hook up."

Maybe this party would be a good place to cut loose.

I've always wanted to seriously make out with a guy, but haven't had the chance. Nothing is stopping me tonight. And honestly, after seeing Roxy, I want to have some fun and take the edge off.

With a deep breath I tell Sylvia, "Yeah, I'd love to meet some guys. Introduce me?"

Superman

Sylvia leads me off campus.

Berkeley is quite hilly. I feel like we're going up and down, up and down. Plenty of people ride skateboards to get from point A to point B, but I can't see myself doing that.

San Francisco is just across the bay, but I can't see it through the fog on the brisk walk to the basketball house. Lit up with lights, music blares from inside, and cars line the street. The front door opens and laughter spills out.

My heart races.

We walk inside, and I gaze around the crowded foyer. It's about a hundred degrees hotter inside than out. A guy comes rushing up to Sylvia, kisses her check, then pushes his glasses up on his nose. "Hey, babe." He continues on to a couch, where he squeezes in between two other guys and picks up a video game controller.

"Wow, he was cute," I say.

She smiles. "They all are."

I think I'm going to like college.

Sylvia goes to the keg and comes back with two very full cups of beer, balanced carefully in her hands. I take mine and sip. It tastes pretty gross, so I decide to simply hold it. Will Roxy be at this party? I scan the room.

Sylvia introduces me to her friends from the dance team, and then a couple guys wander over to us. Sylvia nudges me with her elbow. She introduces me to one named Dylan, a sophomore who plays for the lacrosse team. He shakes my hand, giving me a friendly smile. I like the way his hand feels warm in mine.

He's so ridiculously cute it's not even funny. Cuter than the guy on Roxy's arm earlier today. Blue eyes, buff body, longish blond hair swept back behind his ears. His hair reminds me of Levi's. Looking at Dylan, I feel a strong tug in my stomach, starting at my belly button and shooting down.

"Maggie's coming to school here in the fall," Sylvia tells him.

"I can't wait," he says, his smile becoming a full-fledged grin directed at me. Another guy grasps Dylan's shoulder, speaking quietly to him. They bump fists and do macho handshakes.

Sylvia catches me staring at Dylan and whispers, "He's single."

I raise my eyebrows, and a sly smile forms on her face.

"He's also very nice," she says. "And I hear he's great in bed. Come find me if you decide you want to leave. I need a second round with that football player." She takes off, leaving me alone by the staircase. Crap. This is exactly what I was afraid of. I'm a wallflower at my first college party.

But when I glance up, I find myself looking into Dylan's eyes.

He's an inch or so taller than me, and the delicious smell of his cologne pulls me into a trance.

I think about what Sylvia said, that once you get to college, most people don't have relationships. They hook up. I don't want to leave for college without some experience.

Besides, lately, I've been getting these *urges*. Sometimes I will see this hot actor who plays a werewolf on TV or some sexy musician dancing, moving his hips, and I get all hot and bothered. Sure, I can touch myself, but it never seems to work right. It feels nice, but I don't think I've had an orgasm, and it seems like I'd know. Anyway, I'm always left wanting. I have those *urges*, and I don't know how to satisfy them. I think I need a boy to do it. Georgia agrees.

She says there's nothing like a guy kissing you *everywhere*.

And god dammit, I want a guy to kiss me *everywhere*.

I smile at Dylan.

He smiles back.

And then the worst thing ever happens: my stomach rumbles. Loudly. I'm about to die of embarrassment, but he chuckles.

"Hungry?" he asks.

I touch my stomach. "You have no idea. We didn't get dinner before Sylvia brought me here."

"C'mon," he says, taking my hand and tugging me down the hallway. Feeling his skin against mine makes my heart pound even harder. We arrive in a spacious kitchen, complete with an island and a long table that must seat twenty people. Basketball players take up a lot of space. A guy and girl talk quietly next to a set of doors leading to the backyard. Another couple leans against the dishwasher, making out. A group of guys play beer pong on the table.

Dylan opens the fridge and peers in. "We've got the makings for a PB and J."

"Sounds perfect."

He pulls jelly out of the fridge and takes a loaf of bread from the bread box.

I sit on a barstool as he works. "I thought this was the basketball house."

"Other athletes live here too. So do you play basketball?"

"No, I swim."

He pulls a butter knife from a drawer. "I figured basketball 'cause you're so tall."

"It's a curse."

"A sexy curse. Some of the sexiest women are tall. Like Gisele. Or Taylor Swift."

"True. I'm not sure why I said that. I love being tall. It helps me in the pool."

"See? There you go. It's a sexy curse."

I let out a shaky, flustered breath. "Enough talk. Get back to my sandwich already."

He salutes me with the butter knife, then spreads jelly on one side of the bread and peanut butter on the other.

A super tall African American guy appears in the kitchen and peers over Dylan's shoulder. "Nice, I'll have ten."

"Sorry," Dylan says. "This is for Maggie over there."

Bonus points for remembering my name!

I recognize the guy from the basketball game earlier today. He's the team's star center, Robert Charles. People were saying he'll be an early pick in the NBA draft.

Robert eyes my sandwich and asks in a deep voice, "Hungry?"

"Always," I reply, which makes Dylan chuckle. He's easy to talk to. He makes a girl food. What's not to like?

So after I finish my sandwich—I was in dire need of a snack—I take a deep breath and give Dylan the lamest, but most to-the-point line ever. "Want to get out of here?"

He beams, and his hotness increases tenfold.

Abandoning our dirty plates, he leads me out of the kitchen to the stairs. It's hard to control my breathing. It's been two years. Two years since I've kissed a guy. I walk faster as he tugs me along. I don't even care that we're not talking.

He ushers me to a room on the third floor.

I take in the plush couch, comfortable-looking bed covered with a black comforter, and picture windows overlooking the bay.

"This is nice," I say.

"Yeah, I love this house."

He flips a switch, and a bright white glow illuminates the

room. I squint. Why do we need lights? He knows I want to make out, right? Not read aloud to each other.

"Can we turn off the lights?" I ask.

"But you're so beautiful. I want to see you."

Sigh. A romantic. I always hoped my first time would be with a gentleman.

He steps toward me, gently lowering his mouth to mine. The kiss is warm and sweet. The hard planes of his torso press against my softness. My heart slams against my chest.

"This okay?" he whispers.

"Yes." *It's very, very okay.* I love his smell, the solid warmth of his chest, his kissing style. We relax onto the bed. He deepens the kiss, and I let out a little moan. "Mmmm."

And suddenly, something inside him snaps.

Everything speeds up.

Speeds up in strange way.

His rips off his shirt. "You like that, baby?"

Is he joking? I barely have time to ponder that before his mouth is at my ear and he's panting hard, like he just sprinted a mile. He gyrates his hips against mine.

Then he starts making weird groaning noises. "Uhhhhh. Uhhhhh."

Jesus, what's wrong with this guy? The good news is my muscles are so strong I could probably bench press him right off me.

"Dylan? Um, what are you doing?"

"I'm pleasing you." He puffs out his chest. "I've been told I'm very good at it."

Oh my god. Pompous much?

His erection presses against me, but it's not that enjoyable. God, my life just turned into a really bad porno. Or so I would imagine, you know, if I watched pornos. Did Sylvia really say she heard this guy's great in bed?

"Uhhhh!" he moans.

Okay, that's enough. I start to do my bench press move when he kisses my neck, and it feels nice. Really nice. I could get used to this. Maybe this is what Sylvia was talking about?

But then it gets strange again when he extends my arms above my head, twining our fingers together. "You want more, baby? Oh yeah, oh yeah! You're my little sexy ninja."

Ninja?!

Grind, grind, grind.

I'm pretty sure this won't give me my first orgasm.

He suddenly pulls away to kneel above me. His fingers go to the button of his khaki pants. He unzips them to reveal Superman underwear. I am not kidding. He's wearing briefs emblazoned with a big red S.

"This is moving a little fast… Maybe we should go back to kissing," I say, because this is truly weird.

"You're right," he says, breathing hard. "We should take care of your needs first."

I flip my hair to the side and give him a small smile. "Well, I guess that would be okay if you want to do something for me."

He leans over and kisses me again. His tongue gently sweeps inside my mouth. Wow, he's a good kisser. And I do like his long hair; I run my fingers over his head. But what the hell is up with the rest of him?! Maybe I need to give him a chance. I mean, it's cool he wants to take care me first.

Then he gets onto all fours like a cat and scoots to the middle of the mattress. "Spank me."

"What?!"

"Spank me."

"Dylan, um, thanks, but maybe we could save that for another time?" *Like, never.*

"I get it," he says, pausing to peck my lips. He pushes me back onto the bedspread, lowering his body to mine. I enjoy his warmth against me, but how can I take this seriously when he's full-on grinding me in Superman briefs?

"You want the main course, huh?" he says. "You want a thick—"

Thrust.

"Juicy."

Thrust.

"Steak."

Thrust.

"Dinner."

"Oh my god! That's enough," I say, and push him and his overactive pelvis off me. "Sorry, I'm not into this."

"Okay," he says, disappointed, raising his hands. "I understand."

I get up to leave, glad he was respectful of my wishes.

That's when I hear the noise. Someone's jiggling a key in the door.

Dylan's eyes grow wide. He leaps to his feet, grabbing his shirt and pants. "We have to get out of here. Now."

"What? Why?"

"This isn't my room."

"This isn't your room!"

He shrugs. "I like it better than mine."

Dylan brought me to a room that's not his.

I dart out of the bedroom, past a confused Robert Charles standing in the hallway with a girl, and flee down the stairs back to the party.

What.

Just.

Happened?

$\sim\!\sim$

"Wait, wait, wait. Let me get this straight," Levi says. "He took you to a bedroom that wasn't *his*?"

Hunter and Georgia die laughing again.

When I got home from California late Sunday night, I sent my friends a 911 text that said *I need to discuss an incident!!!!!*

and they agreed to blow off first period Monday morning to meet for second breakfast at Foothills Diner.

Hunter and Georgia are sitting on the other side of the table from Levi and me, and they've been cracking up for five minutes straight. Jerks. I rip apart my English muffin, stuff a bite in my mouth, and chew angrily.

But then I remember how we were laughing like crazy at Hunter last week when he got caught in Shelby's room with his shirt off, and I start giggling along with them.

Levi wipes tears from his eyes. "It wasn't his room!"

"He asked if you wanted a thick, juicy steak dinner!" Georgia squeals.

"And you think it was Robert Charles's room?" Hunter asks. "When he's in the NBA next year, you can tell people you fooled around in his bed."

"Yeah, yeah," I say, waving a hand.

"Was it any good at least?" Hunter says.

"Before or after he started thrusting against me in Superman underwear?"

Their howls of laughter fill the entire café. Truckers at the counter stare at us. The woman at the cash register shakes her head.

After taking a large bite of his bagel with salmon, Levi changes the subject. "How was the pool?"

"I loved it. The coach wasn't there, but I had a great swim yesterday before I flew home."

"Pierson's one of the best coaches in the country," Levi says. "He'll help you shave off time."

"I wish he could help me before conferences next week," I joke.

Hunter interrupts our swim gossip, "Wait, wait, wait. Can we get back to why you fooled around with that douche canoe?"

My friends start laughing again and can't seem to stop. I put two fingers in my mouth and whistle for them to stop, causing the bushy-bearded truckers to glare at me again.

"I wouldn't call it fooling around—we didn't get that far. But I kissed him because I wanted some...you know, experience before college. I love swimming, I really do, but it's *all* I do, you know? Like, how is it I've never been to a real party until the other night?"

"You want to swim," Georgia says. "If you wanted to do something else, you'd do it."

"But what if I've never even thought of doing other things because swimming always comes first? I mean, I haven't even been to a school dance."

"I'll take you to Winter Wonderland, but I'm not sure it'll impress you," Hunter says, licking powdered sugar from his donut off his thumb. "Last year as a joke, somebody put Crisco on the gym floor and a bunch of people fell down doing the Chicken Dance. That was the most exciting thing that happened."

Instead of going to that dance, I passed out at eight o'clock.

That's my life. When I was younger, I only swam three to four times a week for an hour, but when I turned thirteen, my swim coach, Josh, told me I had what it took to make it big, but if I wanted to do that I had to swim all the time. Lap after lap after lap. Up to ten practices a week. Plus weight lifting. This routine exhausts my body, which means I usually need ten hours of sleep a night. My hard work has paid off—I won a spot at one of the best swimming schools in the country—but it leaves little time for anything else.

"I'm about to graduate," I tell my little group of friends. "And when I look back on high school, sometimes I worry I won't remember anything but swimming and eating."

"Two very worthy endeavors," Levi says, toasting me with his orange juice.

"Maybe you just need to carve out some time for you before college starts," Hunter suggests. "Skip a few practices here and there."

"She can't skip practice," Levi says. "We have the state championship in a month. And then the *big* races start."

I nod. I love swimming. This is my life. I accepted it a long time ago. But then I picture Roxy flirting with that lacrosse player. She manages to be a champion, but still appears to take time for herself too. I mean, she clearly knew how to flirt with that guy.

Hunter says, "If you want to go to a dance so bad, go to a dance."

"It's not that I'm obsessed with going to a dance, guys. I just want a little more life experience."

Levi throws an arm around my shoulders. "But how many people can say they've been to the Olympic Trials? Just a couple more months and we'll be able to say that."

"If I qualify, you mean."

He squeezes my shoulder. "You will."

"I have an idea," Georgia announces, slapping her hand on the wobbly café table. "You should make a list of things you want to do before you graduate."

"Like a bucket list?" Hunter asks. "My grandfather has one of those, but when he read it aloud to my family, Gram just about killed him 'cause it included stuff like, 'Get a lap dance from a Vegas stripper.'"

"Your grandpa rocks," Levi says, bumping fists with Hunter.

"Boys. Stop," Georgia says. "I'm being serious. If Mags thinks she's missing out on high school, we should come up with stuff for her to try."

I furrow my eyebrows, and Levi gives me an anxious look. "George, let's not distract her from the pool."

"Levi's right," I say. "It's not that I want to do lots of stuff." *I just want to make out.*

Ignoring me, Hunter reaches into his pocket and pulls out a pen. He fishes a napkin out of the dispenser. "I am scribe of the bucket list."

"The scribe," Levi mutters, rolling his eyes.

Hunter ignores Levi and starts writing. *Steal a car. Get a tattoo.*

Swim with sharks. Skinny dip. Develop a gambling addiction. Get a lap dance from a Vegas stripper.

Nothing he writes down appeals to me as much as being in the water.

By the time Hunter's done with his silly list, which makes him crack up big time, I know three things for sure:

1. My friends cheered me up after my Horrible Hookup from Hell

2. There is no way on earth I'm doing Hunter's list— swimming is much more important to me

3. After what happened with Dylan, I know there's one thing I need to do

One thing I should accomplish before college.

The one item on my solo bucket list?

Learn to hook up.

New Wave

Levi honks his horn from the driveway.

We live twenty-five minutes from the Centennial Sportsplex in Nashville where we work out, so we carpool every day to save gas and to keep each other company. Plus, ever since my first driving lesson when I accidentally put the gear in drive instead of reverse and floored Mom's car into the garage door, I supply Levi's breakfast in exchange for a ride.

Dad stands by the front door with his eyes closed, still half asleep in his bathrobe. As an event planner, he works late and has never been a morning person. Not that 4:30 a.m. is morning. To most people, it's the middle of the night.

"Have a good practice, Tadpole," he says, passing me a bag of bagels and chocolate milks, one for me and one for Levi. Neither of us likes eating before we get in the pool, but we'll need calories as soon as our laps are finished. Chocolate milk is our go-to.

I give Dad a kiss and jog out to the truck, my backpack bouncing against my shoulder. It's about thirty-five degrees out, but Levi the gentleman is standing there to open my door.

"Morning!" I tell him with a smile, and he grunts in response. For him, it's way too early for speech.

We've been swimming with the New Wave team at Nashville Aquatic Club, or NAC, since we were about two years old. That's where our families met. Levi had a very similar experience to mine: he jumped off his Opa's boat into the lake and started paddling around. He had a life jacket on but didn't need it. By the time we entered kindergarten, we were both swimming with eight-year-olds.

Over the years, many of our teammates quit because club practice affected their social lives. But being at the pool with Levi *was* my social life. He was the only person from school also on my swim club.

But when we were twelve, professionals in the sport started saying Levi was "the real deal" and that he should move from Tennessee to a "real" swimming state like California, Florida, or *Texas*. To get to the next level in swimming, I knew he was going to move to Texas. I just knew it. That's where his dad lives. He doesn't really like his father, but he's always wanted to spend more time with his younger half brother and half sister, twins who just turned thirteen.

I wanted to be an independent girl, but I wasn't sure if I could handle swim club without him. Roxy was gone. At school, these girls Leslie and Maria made fun of my broad shoulders, wondering if I could ever fit in a dress.

Levi would say, "I don't even know who these girls are. Your shoulders look good. They're strong."

He was my one true friend. I cried myself to sleep at the idea of losing him to Texas and sighed with relief when he made a decision to stay in Tennessee because he couldn't leave his mother. We've been fierce teammates ever since.

He and I are different, though. No matter how hard I try to keep a measured pace in the pool, I race against other people. He races against himself. I wish I could be more like him. He's like that person who runs marathons just to finish. I would never run one because I wouldn't win. And I want the win.

Levi's so good, he could swim just about anywhere in college, but he chose Texas because it's one of the best swimming schools for guys. Selfishly I wish he'd come with me to Cal, but I know how much he wants to be near the other half of his family. He only sees his brother and sister once a year at most, generally at holidays, and always feels guilty about leaving his mom and Oma and Opa on Thanksgiving or Christmas. I can't imagine what going to college near his father will be like for him.

When we get to the pool, it's still too early for Levi to talk. We spend about ten silent minutes stretching in the yoga studio, then take showers before starting our laps. Coach Josh has three rules. Number one is always take a shower before we get in the pool. It helps keep the water—and our skin—clean. It's the worst when your nose runs during a workout—that's the chlorine mixing with the germs that wash off your body into the water.

Number two is never swim alone. It doesn't matter how good a swimmer you are, you should always make sure there's a coach or lifeguard nearby.

Rule number three is the hardest to follow: try to improve a little each day.

After my shower, I meet up with the other thirty-five swimmers who do laps before school. Some kids are in elementary school, some are in junior high, and nine of us are in high school and are considered elite and compete on a national level. Levi's the only one with an Olympic trial cut though.

Coach Josh is in his usual shorts, T-shirt, and visor that he wears even when it's snowing. It's still dark outside, and sun won't pour through the windows for at least another hour, but the loud rap music playing over the speakers wakes me up. I put on my blue New Wave cap, pull my goggles down, and slide into the water next to Levi. He's been wearing a black cap with the orange Texas Longhorn logo on it. He's proud he signed with them.

With so many swimmers here, we have to share lanes. I'm always with Levi and Susannah. She's my main competition on New Wave, but I consider her a friend. She is a junior at Harpeth Hall, a super ritzy private school in Nashville where everybody reeks of money. I'll be up against her at conferences this weekend when I swim for Hundred Oaks High. It's kind of funny that we're teammates during morning practices but competitors in the afternoon when we practice with our schools. As soon as high school state championships are over, we'll be teammates 100 percent of the time.

The other six elite swimmers are all guys, and while they're friendly, the competition between them is fierce. They take up the next two lanes.

Coach wrote our workout on a giant whiteboard. Today we're swimming 4,500 yards, which is kind of easy. We're tapering for conferences on Saturday.

"Let's go, Lucassen!" Coach yells at Levi as he does sprints designed to increase speed. "Fewer strokes, kick harder."

Sports announcers love his name. Levi Lucassen. It sounds very worldly and mysterious. That definitely describes him at races. He's super serious before, during, and after every meet. He saves his smiles for when we win. At practices, though, he's a little more relaxed.

Since we're tapering, everyone has lots of energy, and there's some goofing around. Normally we'd be dragging by now.

People think swimming is this boring, solitary sport, but really there's no privacy or quiet at all. When I'm waiting to practice my starts—my dive into the pool—my teammate Jason smacks me on the butt with a kickboard. He's a junior who rocks freestyle, but has always been a bit of a slacker and is the kind of guy who doesn't bother putting pants on when he stops for a snack on the way home. He said his Speedo made an old lady faint one time.

While in line to practice diving, Susannah starts dancing on the pool deck to the blaring music. Levi is serious as ever during his laps, but on a two-minute rest break when Coach isn't looking, he throws himself my way and dunks me. I pop up from under the water with an "Asshole!" and Levi cracks up at my grouchy face.

The team swims for about two hours, until 7:15 a.m. As I'm pulling myself out of the pool, I glance over at the guys toweling off in their suits that leave little to the imagination. Truth be told, it was weird in middle school noticing the guys getting bigger. We girl swimmers whispered about it and giggled, but then one day I realized I had gotten used to it. The boys and their junk: it's just there.

That's when I think about my vow to learn to hook up. Maybe one of them might be a possibility? The cutest one is Jason, but as he's wrapping a beach towel around his waist he complains about a problem he's having with a rash.

I cringe. Never mind.

I towel off, then race to the showers. My first class starts at 8:00 back in Franklin so I need to be quick. Without bothering to dry my hair, I throw it back into a ponytail and pull on sweats over clean underwear and a T-shirt. My favorite accessory is a chunky beige headband that smooths my frizz.

It surprises me when I find Coach Josh outside the locker room, waiting for me along with Levi, who's already dressed for the cold in his puffy coat and knit cap.

"A word?" Coach says to me.

"I'll be right there," I tell Levi, who nods and slips on his headphones and opens his battered copy of *Harry Potter and the Goblet of Fire*. He's reading the series for like, the sixth time.

I will be late to school, but whatever Coach has to say is more important than whatever I'll learn in my Tennessee history class.

Coach leads me to his office, which is full of shiny trophies and pictures of athletes on the walls. His desk is covered by a massive swim calendar that covers the entire year. A large red circle is drawn around March 26th, the date of the Junior Nationals Club Championship in Huntsville, the first long course meet. That's when our season gets serious. The other two long course meets prior to the Olympic Trials, the Atlantic Classic in April and the Spring Spotlight in May, are also circled. Those three meets are my final chances to get an Olympic trial cut.

I take a seat in the cushy chair across from Coach's desk. "What's up?"

Coach clicks his pen on and clicks it off. "Levi told me you saw Roxy this weekend."

"Shit," I say under my breath.

"Were you going to tell me?"

"I handled it fine," I say, but I can tell he doesn't believe that, thanks to his quizzical look. He knows me probably as well as my parents and Levi.

Coach slips his pen behind his ear. "So you'll be going to college with her?"

"Looks like it. Ugh." I bury my face in my hands.

"It's not surprising," Coach says. "You're both good enough to get into the best swimming school in the country."

"I wish I'd known before I signed with them."

"Did Roxy bother you?" Coach asks.

"No, not really. She didn't seem to want to talk to me."

Coach sighs and adjusts his visor. "Just remember, you're a better swimmer than her. Your record's stronger. Don't let her get to you."

I always try to maintain a strong and steady pace, but when I see Roxy going faster than me out of the corner of my eye, I go too fast and burn myself out early in the race. Coach keeps telling me my times are better than hers. And he's right. When I'm not up against her, I swim faster. So I know it's all in my head.

I guess we'll find out for sure next month at the high school state championships.

～～

I've been giving Levi the silent treatment all day.

Normally he and I are fine with quiet, but it's been hours since I've spoken to him, and he totally knows something's up. During study hall in our corner of the library, he side-eyes me as he reads his Harry Potter book.

"What gives?" he finally asks.

"Why'd you tell Coach about Roxy?" I complain.

"Because I knew you wouldn't."

"God!" I snap.

The librarian points a finger at me and goes, "Shhhhhhh!" like air leaking from a tire. Levi gives her a little wave, and she smiles because he's her best customer in the library.

"See, this is exactly why I told Coach," Levi says. "She spins you all out of shape. Last year you lost the damn high school championship to Roxy in 200 back, which is nothing compared to those long course races you won last summer."

I grumble. It's true. Roxy had a strained shoulder most of last summer and took some time off. Meanwhile I swam the best meets of my life. I set the Tennessee record for 200 back at the Summer Sizzler. Coach Josh and Levi are right to be worried, but their concern makes it feel like a self-fulfilling prophecy.

Levi drops me off at my parents' business after weight lifting. I go inside King's Royal Engagements, the party planning business Mom started right out of college. The company is located in this fancy Victorian house down the street from where I live. Mom and Dad had massive kitchens built out back, so it's a full-fledged catering operation, and they do almost everything in-house. Their pastry chef even bakes wedding cakes.

When you first walk inside, there's a chic waiting room filled with books of fabric samples and suggested menus. A TV plays videos from weddings and anniversary parties. The flower arrangements are fake, but it mysteriously smells like roses in here.

I say hi to the receptionist and continue back to where Mom sits, passing by the offices of the junior event coordinators. Mom has a staff of six event designers, a director of marketing, an executive chef who we all call Chef, and a ton of kitchen staff. They cater two to three events every night of the week. Mom's the brains and the logistics behind the operation, while Dad is the creative arm.

He loves coming up with party themes and weird names for foods. For instance, he just planned a Broadway themed wedding. The programs looked like Playbills, and the wedding cake featured a red and gold marquee with the bride and groom's names. He even set up a photo area where guests could pretend they were walking the red carpet.

I'm glad my parents are able to do what they love, even if it is stressful at times, like when one of our ovens broke the day of a wedding with two hundred guests. My parents' hard work has allowed me to do what I love—to pay for expensive pool time and my coach so I could become the swimmer I am today.

I walk into Mom's office and plop down in a chair. She's typing on her computer and talking on her headset at the same time. "It's not too late to change the place settings," she says cheerfully, but I can see the horror in her eyes.

Clients are always making last-minute switches. One time a bride switched menus three days before her wedding, and somehow Mom and Dad made it work.

"Thank you," Mom tells the person on the phone. "We can't wait to see you on Saturday." As soon as she hangs up the phone, she drops her headset on the desk and rubs her eyes.

"Gina!" she calls, and her assistant comes running with an iPad. "Can you call Southern Rentals and switch the ivory silk linens to the blue damask?"

Gina nods and rushes off.

"Ivory to blue damask?" I say. That's a pretty significant change.

"It turns out the bride recently attended another wedding that was in ivory, so naturally she needs something different." Mom rolls her eyes, even though the client is always right. She stands up, smoothing her bushy brown hair back into a ponytail like mine. "Let's eat."

Most days I join Mom and Dad for an early dinner here before I walk home to do my homework and they leave for whatever event they're doing that night. I sit down with them in the dining room where they do tastings for potential clients. They often test their new creations on me.

"What do you think of the King's cashew chicken?" Dad asks me.

"It's good," I say, biting into it and chewing angrily. I'm still pissed at Levi for telling Coach about Roxy. I'm still angry about Roxy in general.

Mom keeps shooting Dad looks. Dad, meanwhile, is jotting notes about the food. I peek over at his notebook. *Needs more flavor. Cook it in garlic butter?*

"Pass the bread, please," I say.

Dad gives me the basket of rolls. "I'm calling them 'perfect pumpernickel' rolls."

"Hmph."

"Maggie, Coach Josh called," Mom says.

Coach Josh is such a busybody.

"Do you want to talk?" Mom goes on.

"I'm fine."

"What's going on?" Dad cuts in.

"Nothing!"

"Why didn't you tell us Roxy is going to Cal?" Mom asks, and Dad pauses with a forkful of chicken halfway to his mouth.

"It's no big deal."

My parents glance at each other. "Are you sure you still want to go there?" Mom asks, concerned.

I don't want to let my parents down or cause them any extra stress. They've sacrificed so much for my swimming career. Until Levi and I could drive, my parents were often catering events until one or two in the morning, and then they'd wake up at four to drive me to practice. And don't even get me started on all the times they would rush straight from a Saturday meet to finish setting up a lavish wedding. Take tonight for example.

They're catering the mayor's cocktail party in honor of his eighth year in office.

"I'm not giving up Cal," I say. "I've worked my whole life for this."

"Damn right," Dad says with a smile, giving me a fist bump. "Now tell me what you really think of this chicken."

I return the smile. Everyone else is freaking out about Roxy, which is the last thing I need. What I need is normal. Lucky for me, Dad gets that.

I change the subject. "Any news on whether you won the bid to cater the pajama party?"

"Not yet," Mom says.

The city of Franklin holds an event every year in April to celebrate industry in our town. The pajama factory used to be the biggest business around here, and a lot of people credit our economy to it. Therefore, we celebrate *all the pajamas*. Sometimes Mom and Dad win the contract to cater the party, and other times they don't. We're the best, but the town doesn't want to be seen as playing favorites by only awarding it to one company over and over.

"If we lose to Musgrave again," Dad says, "I am moving to Canada."

Maybe having rivals runs in our family. I have Roxy. Dad has Diane Musgrave, who always tries to outdo his ideas. When he designed a vintage Barbie-themed party for a little girl's fifth birthday, Diane Musgrave retaliated by turning a client's home into Barbie Dreamhouse.

After dinner, I'm so exhausted I trudge home and barely have the strength to make it through my homework. Once I'm done, I check texts on my phone as I get ready for bed. No matter what, even if we're pissed at each other, Levi and I always text good night before going to sleep.

I click on the message from him: Forgive me?

I write back: Yes, you big idiot. Good night.

Good night, M.

A Proposal

The Thursday morning after I saw Roxy at Cal, Jason carries his cell phone out onto the pool deck.

Coach Josh's three rules are (1) shower before swimming, (2) don't swim alone, and (3) try to improve each day, but I'm pretty sure "don't bring your phone to the pool" will become his fourth rule. The second we're out of the water, we rush for our phones like a zombie mob.

But it's weird that Jason's on his phone *before* practice. I mean, it's five o'clock in the morning. Everyone who could possibly be texting him at this hour is here at the pool.

He comes over as Levi and I are stretching our arms before we get in the water. Jason stares down at his screen. "Uh, Maggie, there's a picture of you going around."

I peer over his arm at the photo. It's an unattractive shot of me staring at the Cal pool with my hands on my hips and a confused look on my face. The caption reads: *Need swimming lessons?*

I groan.

Levi grabs the phone, looks at the screen, and shoves it back at Jason. "Don't show Mags that shit."

"Levi, I can handle it myself. Jason, don't show me that shit."

"Sorry," Jason snaps. "I figured you'd want to know. I would."

Jason tucks his phone under his towel on a bench, then does a running 360 spin jump into the pool. Susannah turns rap music on the sound system and dances her way over to splash into the water.

After seeing that picture, I sigh, not ready to dive yet.

"Can't Roxy find anything better to do?" I say loudly over the beats coming from the speakers.

"We don't know that it was her," Levi replies.

I raise an eyebrow. "That picture was taken last week at the Cal pool, Leaves."

"Okay, she probably did it." He squeezes my shoulder. "But it makes her look bad, not you."

"I know. But I still don't feel good."

"She's trying to rile you up so she'll have an advantage. Don't let her win."

Then Levi pushes me playfully into the pool and cannonballs in next to me. After splashing my best friend to get him back for pushing me, I channel my tension into owning this practice.

Out of the pool, however, the tension races back.

By Friday I can't wait to meet my friends for dinner at Jiffy Burger. I need to relax.

Levi drives us to the diner, where Hunter and Georgia already have our usual booth staked out. They are carrying on as usual when we sit down. The waitress takes our order, and then we start talking about our lives.

"Mom found out that the Tennessee coach gave me a diet plan to follow," Georgia says. "I couldn't wait for college, to get away from my parents and do my own thing, but it looks like my coach is going to be just as controlling as Mom. Ugh."

Unlike my parents, who support me no matter what, Mrs. Layne won't let her daughter leave the house without makeup and thinks eating at Jiffy Burger is a bad idea because grease "ruins your complexion." Georgia used to be an elite gymnast, but grew too tall and wasn't good enough to stay competitive in the sport at the highest levels. That's why she switched to cheerleading. Regardless of what Georgia's gymnastics coach said—that she most likely wouldn't ever make a national or Olympic team—Mrs. Layne thought Georgia should've stuck with it and tried harder.

Georgia's mom married her high school boyfriend, was the star of the University of Alabama gymnastics team, and hasn't aged a day in twenty years. She thinks Georgia needs to follow the same *perfect* life plan, and that requires sticking to a diet.

"How'd your mom find out?" I ask, hoping she didn't hack her email. I wouldn't put it past Mrs. Layne.

"I hadn't gotten around to answering the coach's email," Georgia says, "so she called our house and left a message on the answering machine. Then Mom got pissed because 'a lady always responds to correspondence' and said I need to follow the diet."

Hunter puts a friendly arm around her shoulders. "You look great. Don't listen to them."

"It's not about how I look." Georgia crosses her arms. "Apparently it's about starting healthy habits now so I don't gain the freshman fifteen."

Levi stares her straight in the eyes. "You work out all the time. You won't gain weight. You need to eat to keep your strength up."

"I know," Georgia says in a tiny voice. "Why can't people be happy with who I am? Why am I not good enough?"

It's not only her mom that makes her question herself. Last year Georgia dated a guy who didn't treat her very well. He cheated on her, and she hasn't dated since. It rattled her self-confidence. He was the asshole, but it made her think she was lacking somehow, which is totally bullshit. She's smart, loyal, and beautiful.

When our server drops off our food, nobody moves to dig in.

"We love you," Hunter says, squeezing her shoulder. He's such a great guy friend to her, like Levi is to me. "And we're all that matter."

"But you guys won't always be there," she says quietly. "It's only six months until I start college, and you'll all be so far away…but at least there I'll be away from my mom." Georgia takes a long sip of water, presumably to distract herself.

Music from the jukebox fills the silence that falls over our table.

I wish I had a way of helping Georgia feel better. That's always been Hunter's job. He gives Levi and me a knowing look.

"So I had another run-in with Shelby's dad," Hunter announces.

Georgia spits out her water. "Nooo."

"I knew I shouldn't have gone back to her house, but I needed to see her."

"Did you go in through a secret passageway?" I ask.

"No. Shelby suggested I pretend to be a pizza delivery guy."

Georgia narrows her eyes as she uses a napkin to clean up the water she spewed. "What?"

Hunter shrugs. "Shelby said it would be adventurous." He takes a bite of his cheeseburger.

"How did you pretend to be a pizza delivery guy?" Levi asks.

"You know my teammate Logan? Well, he works for Pizza Hut. He let me borrow his uniform and the sign for the top of my truck."

"Then what?" Levi asks, eating fries one at a time, like popcorn, watching Hunter as if he's a movie.

"I got to her house. She pulled me into the parlor, where we started making out on the sofa. We were really getting into it when her dad showed up—he saw the pizza delivery truck outside and wanted a slice...but I didn't have one."

"You didn't have a pizza?" I ask.

Hunter looks sheepish. "That's the one part of the costume I forgot."

"How do you forget the pizza when you're pretending to be the pizza delivery dude!" Georgia asks.

Hunter squirms in his seat. "I wasn't thinking clearly."

"*Clearly*," Levi jokes, and we all start laughing again.

"But it was worth it," Hunter says.

"For a two-minute make-out session?" Georgia asks.

"I really like her. I keep asking her to be my girlfriend, but she says no since I'm leaving in June." Before he starts classes at the Air Force Academy this fall, Hunter has to complete boot camp over the summer. He leaves right after graduation.

Hunter drops his burger onto his plate, aggravated. "I guess we'll just keep sneaking around... I wish I didn't have to leave."

"You don't want to go to Colorado?" Levi asks.

"I want both," Hunter says. "I want to go to the Academy and stay with Shelby."

Hunter's father, grandfather, great-grandfather, and pretty much every male member of his family was in the Air Force. I'm not sure if Hunter actually wants to join, or if he's doing it because it's expected of him. I'm not sure he can make the distinction himself.

I feel bad for him, but listening to the story gets me even more wound up than I already was. And by wound up, I mean...turned on. It's not normal for your friend's silly hook-up story to turn you on, right? I sigh, wishing I had someone to make out with. Sure, some people exercise to relieve stress, but

I already exercise for half the day, so I need some other way to get rid of this tension.

When I roll my shoulders, I catch Levi giving me a concerned look.

Dinner is over sooner than I would like, but I need my rest before conferences tomorrow. In the parking lot, as I walk to the truck, I stretch my arms over my head. Levi walks up behind me and massages my upper back. His thumbs expertly work my knotted muscles. I peek over my shoulder at him, and he returns my smile.

"Feeling tight?" he asks.

"A little."

He pokes my back. "This knot isn't little. It's bigger than a golf ball. Hot tub?"

"Yesss!"

If there's one thing I truly need in life, it's a hot tub. I'm lucky my best friend has one.

Back at his house, we find his mom actually home at a reasonable hour, playing a game of Scrabble with Oma and Opa in the kitchen. Two empty wine bottles and the remains of a cheese platter sit on the table. Pepper is zonked out in her doggie bed; the hair hanging over her eyes flutters when she snores.

"Maggie!" Levi's family says, and they each demand a kiss on the cheek. I oblige, then sit down next to his mom.

She gives me a sly smile. "Got a surprise for you." She reaches into her tote bag on the counter and pulls out a CD with Jesse Scott's face on it. It's his next album, which doesn't come out for another month! He autographed it: "To my favorite future Olympian."

I squeal and hug the CD. "Thank you."

"I don't know what you see in that guy," Levi says to me.

"Me neither," Ms. Lucassen jokes. "He's going to send me to an early grave."

As an executive at Rêve, she spends most of her time managing the Jesse Scott account, and with that boy's drama, it's definitely a full-time job.

I examine the CD. It's a picture of the country star standing next to a tractor, staring into the sunset. "I love this picture."

"I can't wait to tell him you said that," Ms. Lucassen says. "Jesse's decided that tractors are lame and wants a new brand."

"But all his album covers feature a tractor."

"I love those tractors," Oma tells Opa, who muses, "If the ladies like tractors, maybe I should get one."

Ms. Lucassen says, "Jesse suggested a cover photo of him grilling at a cookout."

I cringe. "That sounds like something my dad would do."

"Exactly," Ms. Lucassen says. "I know what sells. Jesse Scott flipping burgers in a Hawaiian shirt would *not* sell. Standing shirtless by a tractor *always* sells."

Levi rolls his eyes.

"But Jesse did say to wish you both good luck at conferences tomorrow," she adds. "He'll be rooting for you."

"Levi doesn't need luck," Oma complains. "He's got *my* genes." Oma was a champion swimmer back in the Netherlands.

Opa rearranges his Scrabble tiles, grumbling, "He's got my genes too."

"You were a mailman!" Oma says.

"Walking all day takes lots of endurance," Opa retorts.

"Maggie needs to relax before tomorrow, so we'll be going now," Levi says, steering me away from a round of Oma-Opa WrestleMania.

In the powder room, I change into my suit, then I meet him on the back porch, which overlooks their yard and Normandy Lake. Their house is on a prime piece of property and has a private beach. When we were little, Levi accused me of being his friend for his lake access.

"Not just that," I'd say. "You have a trampoline too."

We still love to lie on it in summertime, as the smell of honeysuckle wafts over us. But since it's February, we stick to the hot tub.

I pull off the towel I borrowed from Levi, revealing a navy blue one piece. I have exactly one bikini, but I only wear it to the beach. All my other suits are practical. Maybe I should get some more bikinis for college. I mean, what if college kids spend lots of time in Jacuzzis?

I ease into the hot water. Steam wafts off the surface into the brisk starry night. The air smells clean, as if it might snow.

Still standing on the deck, Levi strips out of his gray New

Wave sweatshirt and track pants down to black jammers. It's weird seeing him in those; normally he wears Speedos at the pool like the other guys. His other suits must be in the wash.

He slides in next to me and stretches his arms over the edge of the hot tub on either side of him. It seems like every day his muscles are getting bigger and bigger. I see him without a shirt on all the time, but here in the dark, suddenly his buff body and long blond hair reminds me of what happened with Dylan. I clear my throat.

"What?" Levi asks.

"I was just thinking about that weird guy at Cal."

"Your thick, juicy steak dinner boy?" Levi says, flashing me a smile.

"Would you shut up about that?"

"You brought him up." Levi throws his head back and looks up at the moon. Wispy clouds are floating in from a distance, stark white against the black sky.

"Why were you thinking about him?" Levi asks.

"I'm kind of pissed it didn't work out."

"Guy seems like a loser to me, Magpie. I'd never take a girl to a place where she wouldn't feel safe."

"You're right, it was lame. It's that…I was hoping before college I could fool around with somebody."

Levi turns his head to look at me. "You gonna look for a boyfriend?"

"No, nothing that serious. You know I don't have time for

that. I just want to know what I'm doing when I get to college. Like, I don't want college guys to think I'm a loser."

"You're not a loser. Besides, guys are easy to please."

I want to hook up, but like Levi said, I want to do it in a situation where I feel comfortable. I don't want a repeat of the *thick, juicy steak dinner*. Levi would never bring a girl to a room that wasn't his.

A guy like Levi would take care of me.

Cool gusts of air rustle the trees and blow his scent in my direction. Like me, he always smells of chlorine, but there's also cinnamon gum and his shampoo. It reminds me of cedar. I look over at him. His head is tipped back as he stares at the sky, lost in a comfortable silence. He really is cute.

That's when I picture it. Him lying on top of me, kissing my neck.

The thought sets my skin on fire, flushing my body with heat, and it's not because of the hot tub.

Holy crap, I've never thought about him that way before.

The vision switches from Levi kissing my neck to me unbuttoning his jeans, revealing Superman underwear.

Ack! I clench my eyes shut. What the hell is wrong with me? Did I just superimpose Levi's face over Dylan's in a weird, sexy daydream? I really must need to relax.

I shake my head, trying to clear my thoughts. But my imagination runs back to the idea of Levi pressing his forehead to mine as he teaches me what guys want.

He would whisper, *"Touch the Superman logo."*

I squirm uncomfortably in the hot tub. Steamy water splashes over the side onto the porch.

"Oh my God," I murmur.

His eyes narrow. "What's wrong?"

"Nothing." My voice cracks.

"Bullshit."

"Can you just talk to me about something?"

"Like what?"

"Anything."

"Did you see how Tom Brady was accused of breaking into Aaron Rodgers's house to steal the Packers' playbook?"

Levi starts rambling on about the Patriots, and my mind wanders again. This time I imagine rolling around in bed under the covers with him. Naked.

How would it even start? Would I climb in his lap? Would I just ask him?

"Maggie," he says loudly.

"What?"

"I thought you wanted to talk. You're ignoring me."

"Sorry. I was thinking …" If I can't talk to Levi, who can I talk to? "I want to learn how to fool around."

He furrows his eyebrows. "It's not really something you learn. You pick up your own style over time."

"Like swimming?"

"In a way, I guess. There's a rhythm to it." A grin breaks out across his face. "But it's a lot more fun than swimming laps."

"Could you give me some pointers?"

"Huh?"

I see now I can't beat around the bush. "I want you to teach me to hook up."

The smile disappears. His Adam's apple shifts as he swallows. "What?"

My voice shakes. "You heard me."

"What do you mean, 'teach you to hook up'? You want me to draw some diagrams?"

"No…I want you to demonstrate."

He looks at me. Looks into my eyes. Then his eyes slide to my chest.

"Stop staring at my boobs."

"It's your fault."

"How is it my fault you're ogling my chest?"

"You're the one who asked me to be your sexual Jedi Master."

"Oh my God, you did not say sexual Jedi Master."

"You can't fault a guy for getting a little boob action."

Boob action? What is wrong with him? He's probably saying silly things to try to distract me while his mind races. That's how his brain works.

"I didn't say anything about a sexual Jedi Master," I say. "I asked you to teach me how to fool around."

"We can't. That's *swimcest*."

What Levi means is that Coach Josh would kill us. He is very much against New Wave kids dating. For instance, last year Susannah was dating this older swimmer, Lucas, who wasn't as serious about swimming as she is. He was always trying to get her to blow off practice, and as a result she swam horribly last year. Ever since they broke up, she's been at the top of her game. And one time a couple years ago, two swimmers hooked up for a while and they were all over each other in the pool, which nobody wanted to see. Not even pervy Jason. After the couple broke it off, things got very awkward between them at practice, and they refused to share a lane. Which, again, nobody wanted to see.

Still, we have hormones and spend a lot of time together wearing practically no clothes, so Coach understands that people are bound to fool around. But nevertheless, he'd probably kill us.

"I was being serious," I tell Levi. "I want you to teach me."

Deep in thought, he runs both hands through his blond hair. "Why?" he finally asks.

"I trust you," I say. "You're my best friend."

"That doesn't mean we should hook up… You should wait until you're with a guy you care about."

"This girl I stayed with at Cal told me that no one in college wants serious relationships."

"*No one?*"

71

"Well…what if I don't meet anybody? Or don't have time for a relationship? I want my first time with a guy to be special."

His eyes flash when I say that. "You think it would be special with me? I think it would be awkward as hell."

I push his shoulder. "Don't call me awkward."

"You're not awkward. *It* would be awkward."

"Why do you think that?"

"Because our moms gave us baths together."

"So we've got the nudity part out of the way." I wink at him, and he scowls. "It would be special because I already care about you as a friend," I add.

"I don't think we should," he says. "You'll have to find another gigolo to play with."

"Gigolo!" I splash him. "You are disgusting."

Smiling, he wipes the water off his face. When he looks back at me, his expression is serious again. He breathes deeply. "Maggie, I want to help you, but I don't want it to be weird between us."

I can see the gears working in his head. It occurs to me that being physical with a person isn't supposed to involve a lot of thought, but that's all he's doing: thinking. That's not so sexy. But I don't need this to be sexy.

I tell him, "I want to learn how to hook up, but I need it to be personal and something I won't regret."

His eyes don't meet mine when he responds. "I'll think about it."

Swim Lessons

In order to decide who gets to swim at regionals in two weeks, eight middle Tennessee high school teams are competing at conferences today.

While I do not expect this to be a super difficult meet, these races set the tone for regionals and the state championship, not to mention my club's long course season, which starts next month with Junior Nationals. Long course—what's used in the Olympics—is measured in meters. The pool is a lot bigger too. Today's short course meet is measured in yards.

As usual, Levi picks me up for the meet. It's 7:00 a.m., later than our usual 4:30, but he's still not in a talkative mood yet. "Hi," he grunts, opening my door for me. I'm grateful he doesn't say anything else, because I have no interest in rehashing that mortifying discussion from last night.

Once we get to Hendersonville to the meet, we separate to go to our respective locker rooms. After struggling into my super tight racing suit, I take a shower, put my sweats back on, and go do stretches in the warm hallway leading to the pool, listening to classical music on my iPod to get myself in the zone. I glance around to find Levi. He's talking with a pretty blond swimmer from another school. She moves closer to him, placing a hand on his chest. Are they making plans to meet under the bleachers during down time?

My face flushes when I remember how I propositioned him last night. Shit. What was I thinking? The blond girl's hair is so sleek. I run a hand over my bushy hair pulled back in a frizzy brown bun.

I pull my legs to my chest and rest my head on my knees, working to keep my mind on the violin music pouring from my earbuds.

Somebody taps my knee. I look up to find Coach Josh. He's not in charge of my high school team, but he tries never to miss one of our meets because my high school coach, Mrs. Keller, is more of a sponsor than a coach. She just doesn't have the same level of expertise.

"You're up," Coach says, pulling me to my feet. "Go out there and kill it, understand?"

I nod, and get in line with the other seven swimmers I'm competing against in prelims. I adjust the back of my suit through my warm up pants, making sure I don't have a wedgie.

As I walk out onto the deck, the announcer says my name. "Maggie King! Maggie holds the Tennessee club swim record for 200-meter backstroke after her win at the Summer Sizzler last year." Waving to the cheering crowd, I spot my parents sitting with Ms. Lucassen, Oma, and Opa.

I shed my sweats and test the cool water on my arms and legs. With my goggles and cap securely in place, I hop down into the middle lane and get ready to push off. When I look up to the deck, Levi is standing right above me. His silver chain with the Make Waves pendant is swinging back and forth.

"Let's go, Maggie!" he shouts, already clapping. I give him a nervous smile.

The buzzer sounds. I launch off and start my fluid backstroke. One arm after the other, I keep my body as straight as possible. I spot a girl out of the corner of my eye, so I speed up to go faster than her. I do okay in these short courses, but it's not like swimming in an Olympic-sized pool. The shorter the pool, the easier the swim is for sprinters because there are more opportunities to push off the wall between laps. But I'm no sprinter. I'm better at long distances because I have great endurance between turns. Still, I swim as fast as I can in this small pool.

Like Coach told me, I kill it. After four laps, I touch the wall, finishing the race, and immediately swivel around to check the score. First place! "Eee!" I scream. This means I'll be in the final later today.

After hugging the other swimmers, I hop out of the pool to hug Coach Josh and Levi, then jump around and wave at my parents.

As soon as my high starts to wear off, Coach pulls me aside to do what he does best. "You have to stop racing, Maggie."

"But it's a *race*."

"You know what I mean. You can't go out so fast like that. You know you don't have early speed. You have to stay steady or you're gonna waste all your energy. You need to pace yourself."

I nod as he pats my back. This is always his main critique. It's the reason I always lose against Roxy: I go too fast at first and wear myself out. I *am* faster than all of these girls, but only if I keep a measured tempo. I have strong back half speed. When I saw the girl to my right swimming faster than me, I sped up, even though I knew it would wear me out more quickly. I need to learn patience. Focus.

Coach always says, *"Sheer talent only gets you so far. You have to hone it."*

Later Levi will swim both 100 and 200 breaststroke, and me 200-yard free, which isn't my favorite, but I'm pretty good at it. Since we're still so young, Coach makes us race in all the strokes to see if we might break out and win, but Levi and I are set in the strokes we like. We have some time before those races, so he and I go sit in the stands to cheer on kids from school and New Wave.

Between events, Levi plays Candy Crush on his phone.

I lean closer to see his screen—well, as close as I can. His copy of *Harry Potter and the Order of the Phoenix* is on the bench between our thighs. "What level are you on now?"

He doesn't reply as he continues to tap his phone screen.

"Levi?"

"What?" he snaps.

"I asked what level you're on."

"You *know* I'm on two-oh-nine."

"Who was that girl you were talking to earlier?" Shit. That just popped out. I probably sound desperate. I wait for an answer, but he shrugs and grunts like a caveman.

I should come up with a name for that rude gesture. Shrunts? Grugs? Whatever it is, it's unlike Levi to blatantly ignore me. He's usually over his morning grumpies by now.

Jason from our club team comes and sits down on the other side of Levi, and they bump fists. "I fucked up my turn," Jason complains. "I lost half a second."

"I saw that, man," Levi replies. "That's rough."

"My dad's gonna kill me," Jason says. "He'll compare me to you again."

Coach Josh sometimes accuses Jason of slacking off in the pool. His dad is CEO at a healthcare company. I bet he'd work twenty-three hours a day if he could, and he thinks Jason should too. Jason's a wonderful swimmer—dead fast in the pool—but I'm not sure he likes swimming as much as Levi and I do, and he might be a little burned out.

Levi tells him, "Remind your dad how I messed up last year when my goggles fogged up and I had to swim with my eyes closed."

They do a guy handshake. "Good idea. Thanks, man."

"I remember that," I say to Levi. "I still can't believe you came in second, even with your eyes closed."

Levi grunts.

He has no problem talking to another guy but is cool toward me? This has to be about last night.

Awkward. Instead of trying to engage in further conversation, I pretend to pay extra careful attention to the races, so Levi won't know I'm freaking out inside. Asking him to hook up was so stupid.

In the evening, I win the 200 back final, making sure to keep a measured pace. This means I'm going to regionals for backstroke. One step closer to state.

I do horribly in butterfly and breaststroke, but I come in second place for 200 free, which I was not expecting! Coach comments that my times are getting better and better in free.

Later, Levi swims 100 breaststroke, winning it in fifty-four seconds flat. He seems to forget he was weird with me earlier because he gives me a big bear hug and we celebrate together. I love it when he wins because his smile is so huge, and it's always directed at me.

But when we head to the locker rooms, I find the blond girl from earlier waiting for him.

"Congratulations!" she says, flinging herself into his arms. He glances at me over her shoulder.

I take a deep breath, avoid his eyes, and go grab a cold shower.

Well, I'm exhausted.

Exhausted, and weirded out.

When Levi dropped me off after the meet, both of his hands

iron-gripped the steering wheel as he said, "Have a good evening." Normally he says bye and speeds off. But he sat there awkwardly. *Have a good evening?*

I can't blame him. I did proposition him to teach me how to fool around. We've always been so open and honest with each other, I figured it would be fine. He would say yes or no, and then we would move on. But instead he said, "I'll think about it" and was silent most of the day. Well, except for telling me to choose the music in his truck.

But even that was hard. I couldn't pick Taylor Swift, because what if he thought I was trying to get him in a romantic mood? Or what if I chose Nicki Minaj with her sex lyrics and he thought I was trying to seduce him? So we ended up driving in silence, which was even more awkward than if "I Wanna Sex You Up" had come on the radio.

"I'll pick you up at noon tomorrow," he said. We swim on Sunday afternoons because Coach would never make us practice in the morning because of church.

"I'll see you then," I told Levi, and he nodded once, clenching that steering wheel. My heart panicked because he looked everywhere but at me today.

Once I was safely out of the truck, Levi drove off, leaving me standing alone in my driveway.

And here I am. God, why did I proposition him? Did I inhale glue and not know it?

I trudge inside for a snack of peanut butter and an apple. I should start on my homework, but I decide to veg in front of the TV. I'm glad I have something to concentrate on besides how I made an ass of myself in front of my best friend.

It doesn't distract me for long. The memory of propositioning him keeps popping into my head. I cover my face with a throw pillow and groan into it. What was I thinking?

That's when I feel my phone buzzing under my butt. I scramble to look at the screen. Levi texted.

Can you come over? Need to show you something.

I don't want to seem eager to see him, so I wait a bit before walking down the street to the office to ask Mom for a ride to his house. I spend half an hour fidgeting, trying to avoid imagining Levi in Superman boxer briefs.

Seriously, what is wrong with me?

When I get there, he's out on the wraparound front porch with Pepper. I fully expect him to say something like, "Hello, Margaret. Welcome to my home," in a ridiculous butler-esque voice, like *have a good evening*, so I'm happy to discover he's excited and acting normal.

"You have to see this," Levi says, hurrying me toward the lake, shining his flashlight to lead the way. The dog trots beside me on her leash.

A stone wall separates Levi's land from the small beach abutting Normandy Lake. We've always enjoyed sitting on the wall and throwing rocks into the water, with Pepper running back and forth along the bank.

"Over here." Keeping a firm grip on the dog's leash, he leads me to a sunken area near the stone wall. Looks like Pepper's been digging in the sand. I peer down into the hole, finding dozens of leathery beige eggs.

"Those better not be from a snake," I exclaim.

"I think Martha laid them."

We laugh. This enormous snapping turtle we call Martha has been terrorizing Normandy Lake for longer than we've been alive. More than once, when Martha's gotten ornery with Pepper, Levi's had to chase her off with a rake handle.

"Turtles bury their eggs in the sand," Levi explains. "I guess Pepper could smell them and started digging." He pulls out his phone and shows me a website he'd been looking at. Together we read about snapping turtles.

"When will they hatch?" I ask.

"Not sure. It says about three to four months, so it depends on when she laid them. It's unusual that she laid eggs this early in the year, but it's been warmer than normal, and it says a turtle can hold on to sperm for years until she's ready to have babies."

"Ew. She went to the turtle sperm bank, huh? Where *is*

Martha?" I ask, looking around the swampy reeds. "Shouldn't she be watching her eggs?"

Levi shakes his head. "I looked it up. Apparently snapping turtles don't do anything for their young."

"Jerks."

We smile at each other, then he smooths his hair back. He goes quiet, like early-morning Levi.

"I came out here to think," he says finally. "That's when Pepper found the eggs."

"What were you thinking about?"

His eyes find mine. "You. What you asked last night."

I worry on my lower lip. "And?"

He lets Pepper off her leash, and she immediately begins to streak toward the eggs again. "Pepper, no!" Levi snaps his fingers and points toward the lake.

The dog barks, then darts down the bank, her gray and white hair flopping around like a mop. While she's distracted, Levi and I scoop sand back on top of the eggs, reburying them. Then we sit down on the stone wall and stare at the black expanse of water, moonlight streaking across its surface. He flicks his flashlight off. Pepper's barking mixes with the lapping water, punctuating the silence between us.

Finally he says, "You know I hook up with girls at meets."

My voice is quiet. "Yeah."

"Sometimes I need to relax. To take the edge off."

"You've mentioned that before."

"It's not because I want a girlfriend or anything."

"Okay…"

"What I'm saying is, I can understand why you are interested in fooling around with somebody."

I clear my throat. "Yeah, I've been having these *urges*—"

"Oh my God,"—he shifts his weight as if uncomfortable— "please don't tell me about your urges right now. I'm trying to have a serious conversation."

I can't help but snort, which gets him laughing too. Then he quiets.

"I've been thinking about what you asked, and I was going to suggest maybe you talk to a guy from another team when we're at regionals next weekend," Levi says. "But then I realized… I don't want you asking any of those assholes to hook up."

"You don't?"

"No. You're my best friend, and I don't want anyone to use you."

I pull my knee to my chest and wrap my arms around it. "So now what? I stay celibate forever?"

"Yup."

I pinch his bicep.

"Ow. Maggie, I told you I want to help you, but I don't want things to get weird between us."

Wind blows through the trees, rustling the branches gently. "So let's make a pact that things won't get weird."

"We can say those words, but what if it happens anyway?"

I get what he means. People can promise a relationship won't change all they want, but that's part of life. Things always change, no matter how hard we hold on tight.

"What if we make a pact to stay open with each other?" I ask. "Like, if things are getting weird for you, you tell me how you feel and we'll talk."

He nods. "Okay. Um, how far do you want this to go? I mean, you're a virgin, right? And I'm not—"

"I'm not sure how far we should go," I say. The temperature of my blood jumps from 98.6 degrees to *volcanic lava*.

I want this. I want to make out. All of a sudden I have the opportunity, but it's with my best friend, and oh my god, am I out of my mind for wanting this? I want control. I want to feel safe. Am I overthinking it? I have a nice, cute guy in front of me, and he's agreed to fool around.

I look up into his eyes, and they're patient and kind. The same eyes that belong to the guy who splits his bagels with me and opens my car door every morning.

So I just do it. I lean forward and press my mouth to his. Once, twice, three times I peck his lips.

We pull away and look at each other. Then he threads a hand through my hair and edges closer to me, bumping my hip with his.

"Where do I put my hands?" I ask shakily.

He smirks. "Anywhere."

"That's not very specific."

"Hooking up isn't supposed to be specific. You do whatever feels right."

I kiss him again. It's warm, soft, and slow moving; his lips feel like sunshine.

Does he think I'm an okay kisser? Does he think this is weird? Will he stop this before we even get started? My shoulders tense.

He gently squeezes them. "Stop thinking so much."

I open my mouth. His tongue sweeps out to meet mine. My hands feel his arms, his strong muscles. I slip my hands inside his puffy coat to grasp his back through the cotton of his long-sleeved tee and trace his spine, because it's a straight line to follow. I've touched him thousands of times as we glide past each other in the pool, but when his hands firmly grip my hips, goose bumps break out across my skin. A shiver ripples through my body.

He breaks the kiss, breathing deeply, our lips a heartbeat apart. A lock of hair falls across his forehead as his eyes gaze deeply into mine. His stare makes the hair on the back of my neck stand up.

"Hunter was right," he says, wrapping his arms more securely around me. "You're a terrible kisser."

I playfully slap his chest in response.

Still sitting down on the rock wall, he pulls me to a standing position in front of him. I always dreamed of kissing a guy under the moonlight. I just never pictured Levi as the guy. I'm not sure how I feel about it. I feel plenty fine about his warm kisses though. Speaking of, he slips a hand behind my neck to bring my mouth back to his.

I'm flattered, obviously, that he's continuing to kiss me. And that he's out of breath. But what happens when the kissing stops? Even though this was my idea, I don't want our friendship to be awkward. How can I want two very different things so badly?

"Maggie," he says quietly, touching his forehead to mine. "You're clenching up again."

"I thought guys were easy to please."

"Oh, I am. It's just, if you're doing this with a guy, it'll make him nervous if you're nervous. He'll worry you aren't into him. Relax with me."

And it shocks the bejesus out of me when he grabs my waist and pulls my hips to his, and I discover the hardness of his body. I guess he *is* easy to please.

We've been kissing maybe two minutes at the most—not nearly long enough—when he suddenly pulls back. Again, he won't look directly at me as he works to catch his breath.

"C'mon," he says, standing up to his full six foot five. He towers above me.

"Why'd we stop?" I whine. "I was getting into it."

He kisses my forehead. "Magpie, you don't need lessons. You know what you're doing just fine."

"But I don't know nearly enough. How do I know when it's okay to make a move on a guy?"

"Yes."

"How do I know when to take off his shirt?"

"Yes."

He thinks it's so simple? *Time to pull out the big guns.* "If I'm giving him a hand job, how hard do I squeeze?"

"Yes." Levi whistles for Pepper to join us. "Let's see if we can find Martha."

He doesn't say explicitly that my lessons are over, but it sure feels that way.

Daydreams

I wake up to the sun pouring in through my bedroom windows.

It's a nice feeling. A rare feeling. Warm.

I touch my fingers to my lips. I kissed Levi.

Holy shit. I *kissed* Levi.

Mom pounds on my door. "Tadpole, almost time for church!"

I groan. I don't want to get up yet. But get out of bed I do.

Levi and Hunter don't go to my church, but Georgia does. We sit next to each other during the service and write notes back and forth on the little envelopes they use to collect offerings, using the tiny pencils, like when you play minigolf, which are in the pews. She tells me about how this guy David has been texting her.

She writes: He's not my type!

Do you like him?

He's cute, I guess, but kind of nerdy

That is true. His glasses always slide down his nose, and he runs track so he's super skinny. His body never fills out his jeans, but his lopsided smile is appealing, and he's very smart.

The last guy Georgia dated was a linebacker named Kevin who definitely filled out his clothes. On the other hand, he cheated on her. David, however, seems like an okay guy. He's president of the student body and always smiles and says hi to everybody in the hallway.

Did he ask you out?

Not yet but I know he wants to and I'm not sure about it. What do you think of him?

I decide to tell her what I was thinking. Great smile. Very smart. I approve.

A grin blooms on her face. She likes him. I can tell she does. But the smile quickly fades, and her expression becomes pre-occupied. Getting cheated on really affected her. We told her that he was the jerk because he cheated, but she still felt it was a reflection on her, that it may have been partially her fault, that something must have been lacking about her if he felt the need to fool around with another girl.

I roll the little pencil back and forth between my hands like I'm heating them over a campfire. Part of me wants to tell Georgia about what happened last night with Levi. We've never kept secrets from each other, at least as far I know. But this feels very private. Telling her could also make things weird with our circle of friends.

I put the pencil back in the little holder next to the hymnals and spend most of the pastor's sermon replaying last night over and over again in my head. If I have a few daydreams about Levi in

Superman underwear, does that make me a total sinner? Probably. I concentrate extra hard during the Lord's Prayer, in case God is offended by my fantasies. Annnd then I go right back to fantasizing.

After church, I ditch the skirt and change into my swimsuit and sweats, and wait for Levi at the front door. I'm a little nervous about seeing my friend. After we kissed, he wanted to go looking for Martha. Yes. The boy used a snapping turtle as an excuse to stop kissing me.

I don't exactly blame him. It was starting to get intense. Part of me even wanted him to take off my shirt, but it was like forty degrees out, and no guy is worth hypothermia.

He honks his horn. At least that hasn't changed. After grabbing our chocolate milks and protein bars, I run out to the truck to meet him. He's already standing outside the passenger door holding it open. I climb inside.

Once we're driving down the road, I decide to take the edge off of the silence by being cheeky.

"So," I say. "Do anything interesting last night?"

After a pause, laughter erupts from him. "I found some turtle eggs."

"Is that right?"

Does he have a smug look on his face?

We argue over the radio on the way to practice. He is on a rap kick and I want rock. We settle by turning off the radio to play Overboard.

I say, "You've got President Obama, Michael Phelps, and David Beckham. Who's going overboard?"

Levi moans. "Can't you give me a girl for once? Okay, let's see. I'd spend one hot night with David Beckham because even I can admit he's good looking. I'd spend a year with Michael Phelps learning everything I can from him. That leaves…throwing President Obama overboard. I can't do that! That'd be an assassination attempt."

I crack up. "So what are you gonna do?"

"Maybe I should throw Michael Phelps overboard. I'd have a better chance of making the Olympic team that way."

"And you wouldn't risk the Secret Service throwing you to the sharks," I point out.

"That's always a positive," Levi agrees.

Practice at the pool is pretty routine, but at the end, Coach wants to see me privately again. Twice in one week is weird. I follow him into the office and sit down in the guest chair. I try to avoid looking at the calendar. The big red circles around the dates of upcoming long course meets glare at me.

"What's up, Coach?"

He tosses his tennis ball from one hand to another. "I looked up Roxy's conference times online."

Since she lives in Memphis, she competes in different conferences and regionals, but we're sure to meet at state. "And?"

"She swam a tenth of a second faster than you in 200 back."

I let out a heavy breath. "Shit."

"No reason to worry yet." Coach throws his tennis ball against the wall and catches it on the bounce back. "No matter what happens at state, you know you're better at long course, and you're more likely to get your cut for the Olympic trials than she is. She gets her strength from pushing off the side of the pool. You're naturally stronger and don't rely on your turns."

"Thanks for letting me know."

He nods. "We have to keep talking through these things. You're the best."

I walk out of the office to find Levi waiting. The second he sees me, he slides his headphones off his ears and drapes them around his neck.

"You good?" he asks.

No matter what Coach says about me being better than Roxy, it won't be true until I beat her. My eyes start watering. "Can we go?"

My best friend throws an arm around my shoulders, and we walk to his truck.

So this is the week from hell.

First, Coach told me about Roxy beating my time.

Second, Levi has an interview with the *Tennessean* on Friday. The newspaper is doing a big story on how great of a swimmer he is, highlighting how he's going to the trials in Omaha this summer. He won't stop complaining about it because he hates attention and loathes having his picture taken.

"I just want to swim! I don't want to do interviews!" he whines, shaking his fists at his first world problems.

"C'mon, Leaves," I say. "You should be proud. No one asked to interview me."

"So I'll tell them to interview you instead," he snaps.

I love my best friend, but we sure can get on each other's nerves sometimes. I'm happy for him, but also jealous the paper isn't doing a story on me. Can't Levi see this upsets me?

Third, it appears to be safe sex week in health class.

My teacher, Coach Woods, is very down to earth and cool. Every day she wears a Hundred Oaks football shirt of some kind. If it's not a jersey, it's a sweatshirt or a long-sleeved tee and jeans. Never khakis and polos, like other coaches at school. I don't know how she gets away with it. *The* Jordan Woods probably wouldn't let someone give her a dress code.

I love Coach Woods, but I don't want to put a condom on a banana in front of the entire class. On top of that, she's timing us using a stopwatch! I mean, who makes their students race against each other to see who can put a condom on the fastest?

"All right, Maggie," she says, hovering above me with that stopwatch. "You're up. Grab your banana."

"Bananas are for eating," I reply.

She ignores me. "The time to beat is seven and a half seconds.

Remember, you can't tear the condom, and you have to make sure it's securely in place. If it's not, you're disqualified. Ready?"

I'm poised with an unopened condom and my banana. "Let's do it."

"Three, two, one...go!" She scrutinizes me as I fumble with the wrapper.

"I don't know why I'm even bothering," I announce, freeing the condom from the foil. "I will never have time for sex."

The room full of girls chuckles. I make terrible jokes when I get nervous, which is now, as I'm trying to stretch this condom over a banana that's pretending to be a penis. I pull too hard and the latex breaks. The class cracks up.

"Arg!" Coach Woods shouts, as if she's a safe sex pirate. "You'll get it next time."

I sit back in my seat and sigh. I hate losing. Even if it's only a condom race.

The bell rings. All the girls stand and gather their bags and notebooks. I go to peel my banana because I'm starving. Who cares if lunch starts in five minutes?

"Nobody eat the bananas!" Coach Woods says. "I need them for my next class."

Sadly, I put my banana back on the desk.

Coach Woods calls out, "Maggie, can you I see you for a minute?"

I hoist my backpack over my shoulder and walk to the front of the room. She's one of the few women I've ever met who is taller than me. Her dad played football and her brother is quarterback of the Tennessee Titans, and Coach Woods herself was a player in high school. She coaches the team here now. Condom races aside, I really like her because she talks to us like we're adults.

"I don't have to do the condom test again, do I?"

"No." She sits on top of her desk. "I wanted to ask you about what you said about never having time for a boy."

I shrug. "It's true. I don't even have time to dry my hair."

"I know how you feel. When I was a senior, I had to spend all my time training. And when I wasn't doing that, I was watching game film or in the weight room. It was tough working toward a college scholarship, so I can't even imagine what it's like for you." She shakes her head, and her face goes from sad to one of wonder. "You're working toward the Olympics!"

It's awesome that people support me. It truly is. It motivates me. But it's also pretty scary. What if I let them down? I let my school down last year when I lost to Roxy at state. What if that happens again? What if that trend continues to the long course meets? What if Roxy gets to go with Levi to Omaha, and I'm stuck in Tennessee watching on TV?

Coach Woods goes on, "I wanted you to know that I figured out how to balance football and having a boyfriend senior year."

"How?"

"It helped that I was dating a guy on the team"—she pauses to smile—"but I also found that if I dated someone who

95

supported me and understood why I practiced so hard, it made it easier to spend time with him. He was willing to work around my schedule."

I think about my friends. We always make time for each other on Friday nights.

"It would be nice to meet someone," I admit.

"I also remember feeling like no one would take me seriously as an athlete if I had a boyfriend."

"Yeah, I understand that," I reply, thinking of how Coach Josh got fed up with Susannah when she was dating Lucas. "I worry that people will question my dedication if I were to start spending time with a guy."

Coach Woods picks up the football on her desk and tosses it to herself. "Well I can solve your first problem right there. Stop worrying what other people think."

"That's not so easy. I don't want to disappoint my parents or my coach."

"I think you'll find they want you to be happy, Maggie. You work hard. You practice hard. They won't mind if you take a little time for yourself." She stops tossing her ball and cradles it to her chest. "Most people are so busy thinking about themselves they aren't worried about other people. It's human to think that everyone is always watching everything we do, but they aren't."

"Even when that person might be going to the Olympic trials?" Coach Josh watches us New Wave kids pretty closely. He's like a CIA agent, keeping dibs on how late I stay up at night and when my muscles are tight. "I don't know if I agree with that."

Coach Woods sets her ball down on the desk. "You're right. It's not always that simple. But I wanted you to know that I once thought I didn't have time for guys, but I was able to make it work."

I smile at her, appreciating she can admit life isn't black and white.

Mine sure isn't.

Levi is waiting outside Coach Woods' classroom to walk me to lunch. When he sees me, he pushes himself off the wall where he'd been leaning and adjusts his backpack and black knit cap.

"Why'd she keep you late?" he asks.

Not wanting to tell him what she said, I make something up: "Because I failed my condom race, and then I tried to eat the banana."

He lifts an eyebrow. "What?"

I wave a hand to dismiss the conversation.

He says, "I heard you announced in front of the class that you're never gonna have time for sex, so why bother learning to use a condom."

I *knew* I shouldn't have said that. Good gossip travels fast at this school. "I was joking."

He holds the door open to the noisy cafeteria, ushering me inside. "This whole hooking up thing is really bothering you."

I shrug a little. "Sometimes I feel lonely, that's all."

"You've got me."

"I know, but I want a little more than friendship." *I want to make out. I want a guy to press his body to mine and kiss me all over. And for crying out loud, what does an orgasm feel like?* "I want someone to snuggle with."

"Snuggling makes me hot."

"Like hot and bothered?"

"No, like sweaty hot. Too much body heat for me."

I smile. "You're hopeless."

We sit down at our regular table by the windows with Hunter and Georgia. After saying hi, I unpack my lunch of pasta and energy drinks. Hunter's already halfway through his sub sandwich, and Georgia's devouring a grilled chicken salad…and some bread and soup. She's way over the calorie count suggested by the college cheerleading coach, but I think that went in one ear and out the other, which is good. It doesn't seem healthy to be that restrictive given her workouts. I follow her gaze a few tables away to where David, the guy who likes her, is eating with the Quiz Bowl team.

I nudge her in the side. "He's looking at you."

"Shh." She focuses on her salad. Does she not want Hunter and Levi to know? I guess I can understand why. David is the exact opposite of us. I mean, he runs, but he's about half the size of Hunter and Levi. She seemed worried about what I'd think of him, so I imagine it's the same with our guy friends. Probably even more so.

Two sophomores drop by our table to say hi to Levi. One of them lives down the street from him, but I don't know her name. I do know, however, that she's grown very pretty as she's gotten older.

"Hi, ladies," he says.

I shift in my seat, and focus on twirling pasta around my fork.

"Levi," the neighbor says. "We got a new puppy!"

"What kind?" he asks.

"A Bernese Mountain Dog!"

Levi folds his hands behind his head and grins up at her. "Aww."

"His name is Patches. Can I bring him by sometime to meet Pepper?"

"Of course. Anytime."

I pretend to look at my phone while Levi and the cute neighbor make plans for a doggy date. It's not as if he's mine, but the vibe between us feels a little off ever since I kissed him. Hopefully it's something I'll get used to, like when you buy a new pair of jeans that feel tight at first, but eventually stretch and mold to your body.

Lucky for me, Shelby Goodwin leaves her table of sophomore friends to come sit on Hunter's lap, distracting me from the girl flirting with Levi. "Hey, you guys." They whisper and flirt for a sec, and Hunter pulls her in for a kiss.

"Want to be my girlfriend?" he asks her, as he does every day.

"Stop," she giggles, gently pushing his chest. She still won't commit to him.

Why can none of us seem to have a regular relationship?

Shelby wraps an arm around his neck, and they start kissing again.

"I'm eating here," I tease.

Hunter breaks apart from Shelby. "Mags, what's this about you telling Coach Woods you'll never have time for sex?"

I groan, then start laughing along with my friends.

Unsanctioned Activities

On Friday night, I have to drive myself to Jiffy Burger.

Normally I'd grab a ride with Levi, but he had his *Tennessean* interview in Nashville, so he said he'd meet me there.

"Dad, can't you take me? I don't want to drive."

My father passes me the keys. "Drive with confidence."

"Drive with confidence? I don't even know what that means."

"Don't go too slow, don't go too fast. Drive confidently."

"You're no help."

"Levi and I can't drive you around forever," Dad says with a kind smile.

"Maybe I'll start riding a bike."

"Coach Josh would kill you. And then steal your bike."

It's true. My coach is so afraid I'll hurt myself doing some unsanctioned activity, he'd probably get mad if I played Monopoly. I could get a hand cramp while counting fake money or something.

"Fine, but if I wreck the car, it is all your fault," I tell Dad, giving him an evil look and a kiss good-bye. I jingle the keys as

I walk to his car, a red Honda Accord. As far as cars go, this is as safe as it gets. It's not like it's a tiny, speedy Ferrari or a cumbersome Range Rover. *It's a sedan.* I can do this. I take a deep breath. Open the door.

Sliding inside, I adjust the front seat and snap on my seat belt. I yank on it a few times to test it. I triple check I've put the car in reverse instead of drive so I don't floor it into the house again.

The speed limit down the four-lane road is forty miles per hour, but that is way too fast. I hover around twenty-five. Cars keep honking at me as they pass. I'm tempted to flip them off, but there is no way I can take my hands off the ten and two position.

Somebody honks to my left. I glance over to see two guys from school making fun of my driving. Both of them have their hands at the nine and three position and are sitting up straight like rods. Jerks.

I pull into the Jiffy Burger lot and try to park between two cars. Turning the steering wheel over and over, I repeatedly hit the wrong angle. Somebody honks their horn at me. I honk back and yell, "Hold your horses!" even though they can't hear me.

I decide to give up on the spot closer to the entrance. I drive around the back of the building, pull the car into a spot, put it in park, close my eyes, and take a deep breath.

I send Dad a text: I made it, but barely!!!!!!!

Next I send Coach Josh a message: My dad made me drive. Can this be an unsanctioned activity please?

Outside of the car, I discover my parking job is horrendous. I'm straddling a white line, taking up two spaces. I'm surprised I didn't somehow take up three. Can driver's licenses be revoked for piss-poor parking jobs?

I pocket my keys and head inside.

My phone buzzes. Coach wrote back: I'll talk to him.

I smile smugly. Coach Josh takes my swimming career very seriously and wouldn't want me to do anything to hurt myself or make myself any more stressed than I already am. *Ha. Take that, Dad.*

When I look up, a man is sitting in our usual booth. He's wearing dark jeans, a gray Henley, brown boots with the laces undone, and a black knit cap. I haven't seen his face, but from behind I can tell he has a nice body. And damn, the urges come rushing back. My mind wanders to condoms and bananas. My blood heats up, imagining hooking up with the stranger. I suddenly need to fan myself.

Then the booth interloper looks over his shoulder and waves at me. *Levi?*

I march up to him. "Why are you wearing jeans and that shirt?"

He scowls down at his clothes. "Oma told Mom I was going to wear my sweats for the interview, and Mom flipped out."

"Your outfit looks nice. I didn't recognize you."

Levi examines my face. "Why are you all flushed?"

"Dad made me drive myself," I say, and Levi goes, "Ohhh."

He buys my "driving made me nervous" excuse, but it isn't

103

exactly true. I can't say I'm blushing because I was daydreaming about fooling around with a stranger…who turned out to be him. Am I going nuts? Breathing pool fumes has finally caught up with me.

I sit down next to him on our side of the booth, more aware of him than usual: How close his arm is to mine. How I can smell that cedar shampoo. How I'd like to snuggle up against that Henley.

"Maggie," he says loudly.

I startle. "Yeah?"

"I've been trying to get your attention. You want to split some fries?"

"Get your own fries."

He grins and goes back to reading his menu.

"Why are you even looking at that? Don't you have it memorized?" I ask.

"I was thinking about getting a strawberry shake instead of a chocolate one."

I gasp. "Sacrilege. So, tell me about the interview."

He shrugs. "I thought it was mainly going to be about swimming, but the reporter wanted to talk about my family."

"What about them?"

"Like, how my mom supported me by taking me to practice early in the morning and stuff… The reporter asked about my dad."

His father is always a rough subject. Levi's dad left when he was two years old and never came back to Tennessee. And while Levi wants a relationship with his younger half brother and half sister, he truly dislikes his father and has never forgiven him for leaving. Levi's mom has never dated again because she was so heartbroken over what happened. Levi even had his last name changed to his mother's maiden name.

"Why did the reporter ask that?"

Levi rips his straw paper into pieces. "Because I'm going to Texas for college. He put two and two together."

"How'd he know where your dad lives?"

"I guess he did some digging before the interview."

I elbow him. "Wow, the reporter actually investigated you? I didn't know you were interesting enough for that," I say, to ease some of the tension coming from my friend.

"The reporter also asked about you."

"What about me?"

"Whether I thought you'd get your Olympic trial cut."

I clutch his wrist. "What did you say?"

He shrugs. "I said you're the one to beat."

I throw my arms around him, hugging him close. He makes a fake choking noise, which only makes me hug him harder.

"Am I interrupting something?" Georgia slides into her spot across the booth.

Releasing Levi, I feel my face flushing again. His face is a little red too.

"No, just talking about Levi's interview," I say, trying to act naturally. I certainly didn't tell Hunter and Georgia about last Saturday night's unsanctioned activities with Levi, and I doubt he did either.

Hunter arrives shortly after Georgia. We order food and start chattering away. All of us except for Georgia, that is.

Georgia unwraps her silverware and places her napkin in her lap, smoothing it. I give her a questioning look. *You okay?* I mouth at her.

"I have some news," Georgia says, and Levi and Hunter stop talking about Hunter's first preseason baseball game that's coming up next week.

"David Cantor asked me out."

I break out into a big smile. "Eeee!"

Hunter and Levi give each other looks.

"Don't make faces," Georgia pleads.

Levi replies, "I like how he always starts the morning announcements by saying what the cafeteria is serving for lunch."

As student body president, David does the announcements every day.

"That's all you have to say about him?" I say. "You like him because he talks about food?"

"Food's important," Levi says. He pointedly looks toward the kitchen for his burger and fries.

"Did you say yes?" Hunter asks Georgia.

"I haven't decided yet. I wanted to know what you guys thought first."

"Doesn't matter what we think," Levi says. "If you like him, you like him."

"You could do better," Hunter says, and Georgia's face turns white.

"Don't be a dick," I say.

"Well, she could!" He turns to her. "You're gorgeous and smart and nice. And David needs, like, two belts to keep his pants up."

Our waitress arrives, balancing a tray full of food and doling it out to us. Hunter and Levi dig in and *then* tell the server thank you with their mouths full. Boys.

Georgia does not look happy. I can't believe Hunter is being so unsupportive. Her self-esteem is already shot thanks to her mother. She doesn't need that from her friends. Thinking of how excited she was in church last Sunday, I say, "I think David's cute and confident. You don't run for student body president if you don't have cojones."

"I'm eating here," Levi says, chewing his burger. "I don't want to hear about some dude's balls."

"Balls, balls, balls," I say.

Georgia gives me a grateful smile.

Dinner is a little strained after that, and I'm happy when it's over. After paying our checks, we leave the diner.

Levi glances around the front parking lot. "Where's your car?"

"I parked out back."

"It's dark. I'll make sure you get in the car okay." After waving bye to Hunter and Georgia, I show Levi where Dad's car is. He takes one look at my horrible parking job and decides I'm not driving again tonight. "I'll drive you home. C'mon."

He gently takes my elbow, sending shivers through me.

I haven't been able to stop thinking about what happened when I arrived at Jiffy Burger a couple hours ago. For a second, I thought he was someone else, and I was very attracted to that someone else. Does that mean I'm attracted to him? He barely touched me just now and my body went off like fireworks.

"You're being really quiet," he says. "Are you okay?"

I clear my throat. "Of course." I try to pretend I wasn't reminiscing about kissing him last weekend. Thinking of it makes me a little light-headed. I roll my shoulders and stretch my arms.

"You tight?" he asks.

"Yeah."

"Need some time in the hot tub?"

I know he means it in a therapeutic manner, but I have other ideas in mind. Not that I want to act on them. But I want to be in the same place as him. Maybe in case it happens again? Not that I want to force it. But if he wants to teach me some more lessons...I'd be okay with that. I know he enjoyed kissing me too—I felt him hard against my hip that night. Helping me learn to feel more comfortable in bed is not a hardship. Right?

At his house, Oma and Opa are watching a movie in the den while she knits and he reads the comics section of the newspaper. Levi's mom still isn't home from Nashville. I change into my suit I had in my bag in the car, a pretty pink and orange one-piece that Levi said he liked one time, and then I'm in the hot tub with him.

I can't stop thinking about our kisses. I want more. It's like craving a soft bed when you're exhausted.

He stretches his arms on the back of the Jacuzzi and tilts his head to look at the stars. Normally he's peaceful when we're together like this, but tonight he keeps shifting his weight, causing water to spill over the side onto the deck. His eyes flicker to my mouth and hold there. That's never happened before.

I bite down on my lip to distract myself from how much I want to make out. I bite until I can't take it anymore. I glide through the water to sit closer to him.

Levi tenses. "What are you doing, Maggie?"

I press a light kiss to his neck. "I like what we did the other night."

He sinks into me. "Me too."

"Teach me more."

His breathing speeds up as my lips nibble the skin beneath his ear. "I thought we already established that you don't need lessons."

"*You* decided that, but I really do need you to teach me. I totally bombed the condom race. If I can't do right by a banana, how can I do it with a real guy?"

"Why me?" he asks. "You're pretty. Lots of guys would be interested."

I blush at his words—they definitely make me feel good. "I'm looking to explore," I explain. "I want to fulfill my urges—"

"Mags, seriously, please stop talking about your urges."

I swallow hard, working to find the right words to explain how I feel. "I need to stay focused on swimming, and you're equally as focused. If I were to hook up with a guy I don't know well, it could get dramatic. He could want me more than I want him. Or vice versa."

"I know what that's like," Levi says quietly.

"Or what if I can't find somebody who's good at fooling around like you?"

Levi smirks a little, and I keep on rambling.

"And if I hook up with someone random, I could get a bad reputation. Or he could end up being a crazy person."

"Like the Cal guy who wanted you to spank him?" He snorts at his own joke.

I give him a look. "What I'm trying to say is that I don't need drama right now."

I kiss along his jaw as I work my way over to his lips. He cups the back of my neck, bringing my mouth to his. After a few soft kisses that feel like lemonade on a hot day, he pulls back to stare at me.

"I'm nervous," he says.

"About what?"

"I like this. But you're the best thing in my life. The only thing in my life."

"That's not true. You've got your mom and Oma and Opa and Pepper. Hunter and Georgia."

"You know what I mean."

I do. I know what he means. He's been my rock since we were kids. My constant.

But…I can't help wanting to make out with him. The pull is too strong.

I slide onto his lap. Any other guy and I'd feel like a giant oaf, but with him, the way his hands play across my back, drifting up and down the ladder of my spine, makes me feel feminine.

"We promised we'd tell each other how we feel," I say.

"And I told you, I'm nervous. I'm worried. I'm not sure if I want to do this, but you're still in my lap."

I swallow hard, and start to move to the other side of the hot tub, away from him, to respect his wishes and maybe rush home to hide under my bedcovers in mortification. But then he pulls me back against him. The water ripples around us.

I touch his muscled chest, look into his blue eyes and choke out, "I thought you were worried."

"I am. But when you moved away from me just now, I realized you'd never push me."

I lean closer to him. "So what does that mean?"

He shrugs. "I can give you a few more lessons."

"Lessons in how to be full of yourself?" I tease.

"You bet."

We ease into kissing again with a few simple pecks. Those tiny seeds bloom into a field of bright sunflowers. He slides one of my bathing suit straps down. Presses his mouth to my collarbone. When I let out a little sigh, he slides his hands to my waist and further down to cup my bottom.

"Can I ask a question?" I pant, my breath ragged. "Why is it you're supposed to be teaching me how to make a guy feel good, but you're doing all the work?"

He gives me a smile that's all mine. "Lesson number one: you'll know a guy's worth it when he can't keep his hands off you."

A New Way to Breathe

The week leading up to regionals, I can't keep my hands off *him*.

We don't touch each other at practice, obviously, but the minute we're alone, I am all over him. Monday night my parents are catering a retirement party at a law firm, so I go over to Levi's house to mooch some of Oma's beef stew.

After we finish second helpings, he passes me a tiny envelope. I carefully open it to find a Batman valentine that says:

To: Magpie From: Levi

I smile. "Why'd you get me this?"

"Oma bought me some valentines to give out at school. I guess she doesn't know that kids don't exchange them past fifth grade."

"Aww," I say. "Now I feel bad. I didn't get you one."

Wheel of Fortune is blaring from the TV room, which means Oma and Opa are properly distracted by Pat Sajak and Vanna White. So I scooch around to Levi's side of the table.

"Here's your valentine, Batman," I say, and press my lips to his. When I pull back to look at him, he gives me a quizzical look but doesn't object when I dive back in for more.

"Am I doing this right?" I ask between kisses.

His eyes flare. "Guys like it when girls take initiative…so yeah, this is pretty hot." He twines our fingers together and tugs me closer so that I'm straddling his lap, his chest rising and falling as he works to catch his breath. But I don't let him catch it—I kiss the daylights out of him.

The next day in study hall, Levi and I grab our usual spot in the back corner near a sunny window overlooking the soccer field. I like this table because somebody etched into it: *math is a tempestuous lover.*

Georgia and Hunter have study hall during a different period, so it's just me and Levi. I'm working on the first draft of an essay for my English class, and he's making faces at his biology book.

"I don't see why I have to do this," he complains. "I already got into college. Besides, I *am* an expert."

"Oh yeah?" I ask.

"Definitely. I've been teaching you all about biology." His eyes sweep the library. No one is looking our way, not even the librarian who constantly shushes me. Levi reaches over to grip my knee, sweeping his hand up my leg, gently playing my inner thigh like piano keys. Mouth at my ear, he whispers, "The knee bone's connected to the thigh bone."

His fingertips leave me trembling in their wake. I breathe deeply, to try to calm myself, but Levi undoes me. Taking his hand, I stand and lead him back into the stacks, peeking over my shoulder to make sure no one's following us. When we reach the books on business, I figure it's safe (because who would want to read about taxes?), and I get up on tiptoes and kiss his neck.

His arms come around me, drawing my body close.

"The thigh bone's connected to the hip bone," I whisper-sing, and he brings two fingers to my jaw, turning my head so our lips can meet. He moans softly as we kiss, gripping my hips. His warm, soft mouth glides against mine. My heart thumps. My knees go weak. My hands need to touch him *everywhere*. My, my, my.

The bell rings loudly. We jump apart.

At first we both make freaked-out eyes at each other, because we got totally carried away at school, but then he starts to laugh.

"Yep," he says, straightening his sweatshirt and smoothing his hair. "Definitely don't need any more biology lessons."

That night at my house, we're sitting on the den couch doing homework. He's reading *Fahrenheit 451* for English and I'm doing my calculus, which I do not understand in the least and I'm hoping will click real soon. Reclining against the armrest, I put my feet in his lap. Yeah, it's forward of me, but he's just so cute and it seems only fair after he riled me up in study hall today. He looks down at my socks for a long moment, then rests a hand on top of them.

We keep working in silence. When I rub my foot along his thigh, he responds by massaging it. His thumb grazes my arch, sending shivers up my spine.

"What are your parents doing?" he asks.

"Event over at the chamber of commerce."

"Do you know how long they'll be gone?"

"Another hour, I think."

He sets his novel on the coffee table, plucks the calculus book from my fingers, and tosses it on the floor. Then he pushes me back on the couch and teases my neck with his lips.

"I have lesson number two for you," he says.

"What is it?" I gasp.

"I'm gonna teach you what happens when you feel up a guy with your foot."

He slides a hand under my shirt. I'm wearing a sports bra, which is so not sexy. Shit. Why am I not wearing something lacy and pretty? He caresses me gently, though, which helps me to relax and somewhat forget about my bra. I pull the knit cap from his head to weave my fingers through his soft hair.

Our lips meet as we get tangled up on the couch. My breathing races when his fingertips trail over my stomach. After pulling the sweatshirt over his head, I wrap my arms around his waist, pulling him as close as possible. His back is strong under my exploring fingers, his skin smooth beneath his T-shirt. My hand moves from his back to stomach, gently tracing that line of hair pointing down from his belly button. It makes him gasp and shudder, and I love it.

He talks constantly: *you feel great, you're so pretty, should we take a snack break?*

I giggle along with him at that one, our featherlight kisses growing harder and more intense.

I'm squirming beneath him and feel dampness between my legs, and it's like he knows because he whispers in my ear, "I'm going to touch you, okay?" His fingers trickle to the top of my yoga pants. My entire body is trembling with electricity. Him touching me down there is a lot more personal than anything else we've done, but my body wants it. I freak out again when I remember I'm wearing cotton underwear and not something silky or lacy. At least they are black.

"Okay," I say quietly, sucking in a deep breath.

"Tell me if you have second thoughts," he says, sounding as nervous—and excited—as I am.

He pushes past my waistband, gently grazing against me through my underwear. It feels so good, better than I imagined. His breathing is shaky as he edges my panties to the side and begins to explore the skin where I'm most sensitive. When he enters me, his finger feels bigger than I figured it would.

"Eee!" I yelp.

He immediately pulls his hand away. "What's wrong? Did I hurt you?"

"Sorry, it just felt a little different than I expected."

We can't seem to meet each other's eyes. He sits back up, putting space between us, his face blazing red and confused.

"Wait," I say. "Can we try it again?"

"You're sure? You should never do anything you're uncomfortable with."

I touch his strong chest. "I want to."

He drags a hand through his hair, leaving it sticking up in places. Without looking directly at me, he squeezes back down between me and the couch. He caresses my back and thighs, trails kisses down my neck and whispers things in my ear: *your body is incredible, relax, do you like this*?

Our skin grows damp as we make out, and a full-body tremor rushes through me. When his hand dips into my panties this time, I'm ready. Wanting. Aching. His fingers move inside my underwear until I'm as shaky as he is.

"Levi," I say, gasping into his mouth. "I need…I need—"

"I know." He gazes into my eyes, a lock of hair falling across his forehead. "You're close."

How can he know my body better than I do? I decide to ignore that he has experience with other girls and focus on right here, right now, until an intense tingly feeling zaps through my body and a blinding, hot white light fills my eyes with stars.

So *that's* what I've been waiting for.

"Wow," I pant, dizzy, and he grins.

I relax against the armrest. He rocks back onto his haunches, kneeling between my legs, and sweeps his hair back with both hands.

We stare at each other, panting like we sprinted a mile.

"Um, shouldn't I do something for you?"

His breathing is still a little frantic. "You already did."

My eyes drift to the front of his shorts. He is ready to go.

"You don't want me to spank you?" I ask, and he erupts in laughter. My joke kills the tension, at least for a few seconds. Then I lick my lips and take another peek at his shorts. I reach to touch him, but he takes my hand in his and kisses my knuckles.

"Not tonight," he says.

"Another time?"

He doesn't answer, just slides down next to me, and spoons me from behind. His warm breath tickles the back of my neck.

"That bad?" I ask.

"Huh?"

"Was I that bad?"

"Mags, don't be silly. Can't you feel how turned on I am?"

It'd be hard to miss the bulge pressing against my lower back. "Then why'd we stop?"

He doesn't answer. He sweeps my hair away from my neck, and lays his chin there, lips close to my pulse. I think about what we just did. I screeched "Eee!" in front of him. I can't imagine how embarrassing that would be with another guy. I'm glad it happened with Levi, someone I feel safe with.

But the experience gap between us is so clear. Levi lost his virginity to an older girl when he was fifteen at a swim meet in Miami. He knows what he's doing. Meanwhile, I'm squealing.

He and I lie in silence until my heartbeat returns to normal, and that's when the front door opens and shuts.

Levi quickly sits up and grabs for his tennis shoes. I twist my shirt and yoga pants into place and pull my hair back into a messy ponytail. His cheeks are still red when we walk into the kitchen where Mom and Dad are bickering.

"I told you no one would appreciate the secret sauce," Mom says. "We're not McDonald's."

"I know, I know," Dad says. "We're—"

"King's Royal Engagements," Levi and I say in unison.

My parents smile at us, and Mom looks from me to Levi, pausing on our faces longer than usual. My best friend's skin is still flushed from making out. Is mine? Mom regards us skeptically, like that time in junior high we stayed out at the lake way past dark and didn't answer our cell phones.

Levi, thank the heavens, breaks the tension. "You got any of that secret sauce left?" he asks, and within a minute Dad is serving him up a cocktail plate packed with tenderloin and a reddish-orange sauce.

Levi tastes it, then starts chowing down enthusiastically. "It's your aioli sauce. Why not just call it that?"

Mom sighs. "That's what I said."

"Because I thought secret sauce sounded mysterious," Dad says.

"Mom's right," I say. "It sounds like McDonald's, which isn't exclusive enough for King's Royal Engagements."

"You could call it 'Not your mother's aioli sauce,'" Levi suggests.

Dad snaps and points at him. "You're on to something."

Mom and I groan.

She checks her watch. "Shouldn't you two be getting to bed? You're gonna be tired in the morning."

Being a swimmer means having the bedtime of an elementary schooler. "I'll walk Levi out," I say.

After he takes a final bite of tenderloin and collects his books and backpack, I lead him to the front hall. I stand in the doorway, leaning against the doorframe. He glances over my shoulder into the house, then leans forward and presses his forehead to mine. Our breath mingles together, hot in the cool February air.

"Why'd you stop me before?" I ask.

"Because I worried if I started I wouldn't be able to stop."

He gives my shoulder a quick squeeze, then heads toward his truck, not looking back.

～～～

When Coach told us a USA Swimming representative was coming to speak with the elite swimmers at our club, he failed to mention the Knoxville Krakens and Memphis Marines were coming too.

USA Swimming wants to keep an eye on the talent all over the country, but it's easier for them to meet with us on a state level. That's why Susan Kennedy is meeting three regional club teams here in Nashville after school today.

Once I've changed into my swimsuit and sweats, I join Levi in the stands next to the pool. His nose is buried in the paperback he's reading.

"Hi," I say, sitting down so close our hips touch.

His eyes don't leave the words on the page, but he smiles. "Hey, Mags." He gently pats my knee. Part of me wishes he'd leave his hand there, to calm my nerves, but he uses it to turn the page in his book, which, based on the cover, appears to be about a trio of warlocks and their girlfriends on a beach vacation.

The heavy double doors to the aquatics center open, and in march swimmers from Knoxville and Memphis, the Krakens in silver sweats and the Marines in green. Roxy leads the Marines to the stands. When climbing the stairs past me, Roxy pretends to trip, ramming her foot into mine.

"Ow," I say.

Levi looks up from his book, giving me a weird look. Then he sees her.

"Hi, Levi," she flirts, moving to a seat directly behind us. We ignore her.

"What are you doing here, Maggie?" Roxy asks. "I thought this was a session for elite swimmers."

"I know, right?" I say. "Considering I'm way better than you, this session'll probably be a waste of my time."

Levi smirks at me sideways.

Coach Josh blows his whistles. "Okay, everybody, settle down.

Everyone put your phones on silent please." Coach waits as everyone quiets. "Levi, put that book away."

Levi grumbles, snapping his paperback shut.

Coach introduces Ms. Kennedy, a woman dressed in a white polo shirt, blue track pants, and tennis shoes. "Susan was an assistant US women's coach for the 2012 London Olympics. We're lucky to have her here today."

As we applaud politely, Levi points out a man sitting several rows away. "It's the sports reporter I met with last Friday. The guy who's doing the story on me."

I crane my head to check him out. Wow. It's amazing that a reporter from the *Tennessean*, the biggest newspaper in the state, is here covering the session with Ms. Kennedy. With the press here, it will be crucial to be on point today.

Ms. Kennedy begins by giving us a pep talk about how we're the future of this sport. "The main reason I'm here is get a sense of your training and make sure your form is correct. Any one of you could be a future gold medalist. The next Michael Phelps."

"Well, not me," I whisper to Levi. "Because I have girl parts."

Levi laughs at my joke, earning us glares from Coach Josh and Ms. Kennedy.

"I can't wait to see the talent here today," Ms. Kennedy says. "Everybody line up by the pool. Before you dive in, tell me your name."

One by one, Ms. Kennedy watches every swimmer swim each

stroke. Jason and Susannah head to the rear of the line. Levi and I end up in the middle, with Roxy right behind us. If I didn't know any better, I would think she's trying to get his attention. And really, who could blame her?

He's hot.

Levi strips out of his blue New Wave sweats. I should be concentrating on psyching myself up to impress Ms. Kennedy, but Levi looks so good in his Speedo. His abs are perfectly defined. His torso is a flawless V. Seeing his golden body reminds me of last night, how he explored me but avoided my touch.

"Good luck," he says to me, before diving into the pool.

Levi demonstrates his freestyle stroke for Ms. Kennedy, moving through the water at a rapid pace. She consults her stopwatch as she jots down notes on her clipboard, looking impressed.

When Levi emerges from the pool, she declares his form "Flawless."

He removes his goggles, smiling. "Thank you, ma'am."

"We're looking forward to seeing you in Omaha this summer."

Levi and I beam at each other, excited USA Swimming is keeping an eye on him.

"Next up," Ms. Kennedy says.

I walk up to the blocks. "I'm Maggie King."

"Nice to meet you, Maggie," she replies with a smile. She makes a checkmark on her board. "Whenever you're ready."

I leap from the blocks into the pool, swimming free like a fish through the warm water. At the other end of the pool, I flip into my turn and change to breaststroke for my return. Next I demonstrate butterfly and end with backstroke. Ms. Kennedy walks alongside the pool, examining my every move.

I climb out of the water, hopeful she'll say "Flawless" like she did with Levi. Instead, she motions for Coach Josh to join us away from the other swimmers. "Maggie, your freestyle looks great. You have a lot of potential there, but I want to see your starts in back again. Can you jump back into the pool and do a few more for me?"

I furrow my eyebrows. It's embarrassing to do this in front of Roxy, but I follow Ms. Kennedy's instructions. I demonstrate five starts, then climb back up to join her.

She's chewing the end of her pen. "Three of those were perfect, but two worried me."

Oh no. This is my favorite stroke. My best *stroke.* "What's wrong with it?"

"When you shoot off backward from the wall, you're a little too high above the water. This is causing your feet to drag. It's slowing you down."

"Oh. I never noticed that."

Ms. Kennedy smiles kindly. "Unless you fix it, I'm afraid you'll spend entire races making up for the ground you lose at the beginning. You've got great power—that's what's kept you competitive. But if you want to reach the next level, you need to improve your start."

"Yes, ma'am. I'll work on it."

Coach and Ms. Kennedy trade ideas, suggesting videos that I should watch, along with some exercises to correct my form. But I've been pushing off the wall the same way for ages. It's like asking me to change how I breathe.

Once she dismisses me, I look around for Levi. I find him gazing over at me. Lines of concern crease his forehead.

Without thinking, I beeline for him and lean against his side. He wraps an arm around my shoulders. "What's wrong?"

"I need to work on my starts in back." I relay what Ms. Kennedy told me. "My form sucks."

"We'll fix it."

"That's like telling me to start writing with my left hand."

"Mags." He takes me by both shoulders to look me straight in the eye. "We'll fix it."

Someone splashes into the water. I turn around to see Roxy's aggressive freestyle racing across the pool. I bite my lip. She's getting better and better.

It seems Susan Kennedy agrees with me. Roxy climbs out of the pool to get her critique.

"Flawless."

The newspaper article about Levi comes out two days before regionals.

We're tapering again today, so we have lots of leftover energy.

Between sets when I'm leaning against the edge of the pool, Levi tickles me under the water.

"Stop it," I say, but he tickles me again.

I push him away.

He dips his head to whisper in my ear. "Want to play sharks and minnows? See, now you're a little minnow swimming along and I'm a big, hungry shark." He touches my waist under the surface where no one can see. "And when I catch you I'm gonna eat y—"

"Maggie, Lucassen, get going!" Coach Josh says, pointing toward the other end of the pool. It's a good thing break is over because my face is on fire at Levi's words. He says the naughtiest things. And I kind of love it.

After finishing my morning laps, I climb out of the pool to find Coach Josh poring over the newspaper. I slip my feet into my sneakers and walk over to him, toweling off at the same time.

"Is that it?" I ask, smiling widely. I can't wait to see what the *Tennessean* wrote about my friend. I reach out a hand to take it from Coach, but he snatches it away from me.

"In my office. Now."

Okayyy. His reaction is kind of over the top. I tried to grab a newspaper from him, not his wallet.

I glance over at Levi, who shrugs at me as if to say, *Yeah, Coach is a weirdo, but he's a talented weirdo, so put up with him, we must.*

I slip my hoodie and pants on over my swimsuit, and follow Coach into his office. Could he have heard what Levi whispered about me being a minnow and him being a shark?

"What's wrong?"

He puts the newspaper down on his desk. "Did Levi mention the article was going to be about him *and* Roxy?"

"What?" I rush to pick up the newspaper. The headline reads *Tennessee's Untouchable Talent.*

"Shit," I mumble, my fingers shaking, rattling the paper as I scan it. The reporter even quoted Susan Kennedy, who said, "Levi Lucassen is on his way to becoming a star, and Roxy Coulter is one to watch."

I find a sentence where Levi said I'm the one to beat, but the paper doesn't mention me otherwise.

"How did this happen?" I ask. "Why wouldn't they feature me? I won 200 back at the Summer Sizzler!" *Of course, Roxy couldn't compete because she had a strained shoulder…*

Coach comes around the desk and places a hand on my back. Together we stare down at the front-page feature. The picture of Roxy shows her standing next to a blue swimming pool, but no one will even notice the shimmering water because she's so gorgeous. She has black hair with purple and pink streaks in it, she's tan, and her diamond nose stud makes her appear exotic. The article mentions how she has ten thousand Twitter followers, and how people love watching the swimming videos and swimsuit pictures she posts. I only have about five hundred followers, and they're mostly people from school and the pool.

Seeing her picture next to Levi's cute face makes me feel sick.

Coach wads up the newspaper and tosses it in the trash can. "I wanted to talk to you about the article before you saw it on your own because you need to hear this from me—the media always gets it wrong. She's not the best swimmer in this state. You are."

I bite into my lower lip. If I'm the best swimmer, why was her time better than mine last weekend? Why do I have problems with my starts?

It's as if Coach reads my mind because he says, "She swam faster than you because you didn't stick to your training. You wasted your energy at the start of the race instead of building steadily. And we're going to nail your starts. Susan Kennedy asked that I keep her updated on your progress."

A smile begins to form on my face. "She did?"

"You bet she did. We're not going to think about this article again, understand?"

"Yes."

I leave his office to hit the showers. A tear slips out of my eye as I stand under the hot water. It rolls down my face. If I could only travel back in time to that day I met her at Normandy Lake. Instead of encouraging her to try out for New Wave, I would go back to playing poker with Levi on a towel on the sand.

I come out of the locker room to find Levi's already dressed in his usual hoodie and running tights with athletic shorts on over them. His blond hair is wet and slicked back, and he's wearing headphones. When he sees me, he slips them off and dangles them around his neck. I don't even care who sees, I walk straight into his arms and hug him tight.

"I didn't know," he whispers.

"I know. They probably chose her for the article because she looks interesting."

Levi edges slightly away from me and glances around the empty hallway, then kisses my cheek. "If we didn't have to go to school right now, I'd show you just how much more interesting you are. You're a minnow and I'm a shark." He playfully growls in my ear.

That night at his place, it sure does get more interesting.

Once we're positive Oma and Opa are zonked out, Levi has me in his bed. He was totally holding out on me when he said I didn't need hookup lessons. Because it turns out I do. I really, really do.

"Do you own Superman underwear?"

He gives me a look. "No. I do not own Superman underwear."

"Oh."

"Do you wish I had Superman underwear? Do you have a fetish?" He starts tickling me.

"Ahhh! Stop. No, I do not have a fetish I just...I just...I don't know!"

He pulls me on top so that I'm straddling him. "Is this your way of saying you want to see my underwear?"

How can he be so up front? Yeah, I'm talkative out of bed, but in bed my voice clams up. I decide to go for it. I reach for the waistband of his athletic shorts.

He pries my fingers away. "Nope. You gotta tell me what you want first."

"But why?" I whine.

"If you aren't comfortable enough to tell a guy what you want, you shouldn't be in bed with him. Okay?"

"Okay…well, I want to do whatever I want without having to ask."

"Maggie," he chides, teasing me.

"Fine. I want to take off your shorts."

He releases my hands from his grip. I tug on his waistband again and he helps me to edge them and his running tights all the way off. He's wearing a pair of dark navy boxer briefs. Underwear are not that dissimilar from swim briefs if you think about it, but this still feels super different. It's more intimate.

With a shaky hand, I reach down to touch him through his boxers, carefully exploring where he's sensitive, and as his breathing begins to race, his mouth captures mine.

"Maggie," he breathes between kisses. Hearing him pant my name excites me, and I reach past the waistband to wrap my fingers around him. His hand covers mine, to stop me from moving. "You don't have to."

"I want to," I say quietly, and after a long look in my eyes, he releases my hand. With a hot flush gliding over my skin, I begin to move up and down again.

"You can grip me a little harder," he pants with a heated stare.

"Won't I hurt you?"

"You feel amazing."

I've never touched one before, and it's not what I expect at all. It's hard and silky...and big. I sneak a peek at it. "Oh no."

He jerks himself to a sitting position. "What's wrong?"

"How in the world would that ever work? You know, with sex...and fitting?"

With a small smile, my best friend reaches out to touch my flushed cheek. "Don't worry, when you're ready to do it with somebody, it'll work."

"Are you bigger than everybody else?"

He smiles again. "I don't think so. I'm normal, I guess." But I notice he puffs his chest a little at the compliment. Boys.

We lie back down on the bed together. He runs his hands across my back, soothing me.

"Don't be scared of it," he says as I take him in my hand again. "When you're getting ready to have sex, make sure you do plenty of foreplay."

My body catches on fire at that word. "Like, handcuffs and whips and stuff?" I tease.

He drops his face into the crook of my neck, cracking up. "No! Not that kind of foreplay. I'll show you what I mean." He flips me onto my back and pushes my arms above my head, circling my wrists.

I free myself from his grip and say, "Nope. You have to *tell me* what you want. You can't just show me."

"You're evil."

I wink at him. "I learned from the best."

"I'll tell you what I want. I want you wearing Catwoman underwear," he says, making me die laughing. "Are you wearing Catwoman underwear?"

He lifts my shirt over my head and tugs my leggings down. Tonight I made sure to wear panties to match my lacy blue bra, which draws a gasp out of him. His eyes scan me appreciatively. He lies on top of me, fitting his warm body to mine, and I wrap my trembling arms around his neck, my legs around his waist. I can't believe we're kissing in our underwear. Being physical with a guy is a part of my life now, and I love it. I feel like a woman.

As I continue to explore his body, he uses his hand to pleasure me again like the other night until a shockwave jolts through me. I gasp at its intensity.

"God, Maggie," Levi growls.

Then Pepper jumps on the bed, noses her way between us, and starts licking my face.

"Pepper, baby girl, no! That's my job," Levi says, and I can't help but giggle as he wrangles his dog off the bed in his boxer briefs. When he joins me again, his smile is bursting at the seams.

I am having such a good time, but it gets even better when he dips his lips to my ear. "This is what I mean by foreplay. I'm going to drive you crazy with my mouth."

And he does.

And oh my god.

Oh my god.

The Most Embarrassing Moment in the Entire Universe. Ever.

The day of regionals, I wake up grinning about last night.

Levi didn't leave much of my body unkissed.

I am very excited about the possibility of doing that with him again. It feels like an addiction. I lie in bed thinking about it, about him, and what it would be like to return the favor and kiss him *everywhere*, until Dad starts pounding on my door, yelling at me to get up and get dressed already.

The swim meet is taking place in Murfreesboro, which is about half an hour from Franklin. Levi's mom is in New York for a Jesse Scott concert, and my parents are catering a fiftieth wedding anniversary luncheon, so Oma and Opa drive us. Levi and I sit in the backseat of their Stone Age station wagon, listening to his grandparents bicker.

"I told you you should've taken I-40, not 24," Oma complains.

"I like 24," Opa argues. "The views are better."

"There's too much traffic!"

"Oma, c'mon," Levi says. "We only had to wait behind two cars to get on the interstate."

Opa swerves into the next lane, narrowly missing a semi.

Levi groans. "If I'd wanted to see my life pass before my eyes, I would've caught a ride with Maggie."

"Hey! That's not nice."

"But it's true."

I playfully cross my arms. "Harumph."

"I have no idea why you put up with my grandson," Oma says to me.

Levi raises his eyebrows and gives me a naughty little smile. He leans over and whispers, "You put up with me because I would wear Superman underwear for you, right?"

"Shut up," I hiss, glancing at Oma and Opa, but once I make sure his grandparents didn't hear him, I smile like crazy. Levi grins at that, and reaches over to give my hand a quick squeeze. He leaves his hand on my thigh, caressing it.

We arrive at the Middle Tennessee State University natatorium and head straight to the locker rooms to shower and put on our red Hundred Oaks sweats and swim caps. I spend some time stretching, doing jumping jacks, and swimming a few laps in the practice pool to loosen up before prelims.

When the announcer calls my name, I walk out onto the pool deck, waving at the cheering crowd. I'm feeling really good today.

First up is 200-yard free. After taking off my sweats and tennis shoes, I shake out my arms, kick my legs, and take a few practice strokes on dry land. I make sure my goggles are in place.

Right before the start, Coach calls out to me, "Maggie! Strong and steady."

Nodding at him, I step up to the blocks. The buzzer sounds. I dive in—quick off the block—and dolphin kick three times, gliding through the water at a brisk pace. I pay no attention to what's happening to my right or left. It's just me and the water. My muscles feel good, like I could go even faster if I want to, but Coach's voice sounds in my mind: *Strong and steady.*

At the end of my final lap, I touch the wall with both hands and pop up to check my time on the scoreboard. Oh my god. I had a personal best today! 1:43.15! It's not Olympic-level, but it's great for me in free. I climb out of the pool and throw myself at Coach for a hug.

"Now *that's* what I'm talking about," Coach Josh says.

I leave his arms and rush to Levi. He embraces me, then we jump around a little, celebrating.

"Let's hope your time rubs off on mine," he says.

I wave a hand. "You got this."

But his prelims for 100 and 200 breast don't go so well; his times are second to Jason's, which is pretty much unheard of for him. It's not the end of the world. He'll still be placed in the A finals, and a second or third place win later today would guarantee him a spot at state.

When he climbs out of the pool after his second prelim, though, he's pissed. He grabs his sweats and tennis shoes, and stalks away, dripping water across the deck. I give him a minute in case he needs to be alone, then join him in a hallway, which is lined with pictures of champion swimmers. He's still having difficulties breathing. His goggles dangle from his hand.

"You okay?" I whisper. "Are you hurt? Are your glutes tight again?"

He rubs his forehead. "I'm just not doing my best today."

"You tired? Need a protein bar?"

"I'm a little antsy. I can't get relaxed."

"Why?"

He shakes out his shoulders. "I guess I'm a little horny."

I blanch at his bluntness. "You mean…?"

"I haven't done it in a while."

"Oh yeah? Why not?"

He shrugs a little. "You and I have been fooling around. I guess it didn't feel right to do that to you."

I never said he couldn't hook up with someone else. I open my mouth to say this, but it doesn't quite feel true. The idea of him with another girl deflates me like a balloon.

Levi and I have time before our finals. It's not like my parents are here. I glance up into the stands. Oma and Opa are squinting at a crossword puzzle together. Coach Josh is talking with my club teammate, Susannah, who I competed against in free earlier. No one's paying attention to us right now. It would be easy to steer him under the bleachers and stroke him with my hands. I could sink to my knees, free him from his swimsuit, and go down on him. The naughty vision makes my skin feel electric and prickly hot. I suddenly need to fan myself.

I turn back to Levi. "I can help you. You know, if you want."

He leans against the wall. "I don't want to use you like that, Magpie."

He's teaching me how to hook up. If that's not *me* using *him*, I don't know what is.

I chew on my fingernail, worried I'm taking advantage of my friend. But I mean, he gets something out of it too, right? We've been having a great time together.

But it was just supposed to be a good time. Me learning some stuff. It wasn't supposed to be me affecting his swim routine. I wasn't supposed to be jealous of him doing other girls. This is messed up.

"If you need to hook up with somebody to take the edge off," I tell him quietly, "I wish you would."

He gives me a long look. Then he rubs the back of his neck. "I can take care of it myself," he says, and leaves me standing there in the empty hallway. Alone.

Why does our relationship suddenly feel like a multiple-choice test where none of the answers are right?

Mom keeps a grocery list on the fridge.

If I need something, I add it to the list and she gets it for me. *Toothpaste, body wash, mascara, lotion.*

Somehow, though, I think she'd give me the third degree if I were to write *condoms*.

So one afternoon after weight lifting, I walk down the street to King's Royal Engagements to borrow Mom's car. I tell her I'm going to the public library for a book they don't have at school.

She stops typing on her computer and turns to stare at me. "You're driving yourself to the library?"

"Yeah," I croak.

"I'm surprised you didn't have Levi take you before he went home."

"I forgot. So can I borrow the car?"

Mom fishes her keys out of her purse, passing them to me. "What book do you need from the library that they don't have at the school?"

"Oh, um, it's for a paper on snapping turtles," I lie.

"Snapping turtles?"

I cough. "Yeah."

"And you can't look it up on the Internet?"

"Mr. Robinson says we can't use any online sources."

Mom doesn't believe one word I'm saying. God, why did I think this would be a good idea?

She passes her keys to me. "Be careful, Tadpole."

I call "Thanks!" over my shoulder and hustle through the front door to the parking lot.

Once I'm in the driver's seat, I buckle up and adjust my

mirrors, and with a deep breath, I start the ignition. Driving to the grocery store seems like a big risk in order to buy condoms, especially since there's no guarantee I'll be having sex. But safe sex is important. Coach Woods said it's crucial to always be prepared. I'm sure Levi has condoms, but girls should have their own supply too.

Before we first kissed, Levi asked how far I wanted to go. I wasn't sure at the time, and if we're being honest, I'm still unsure. But when we kiss, my thoughts disappear along with my clothes. It's just me and him, our bodies, and passion.

I understand why Coach Woods says it's important to be prepared for anything.

I put the car in reverse.

Which grocery store should I go to? Food Lion and Walmart are generally very busy, and several of my classmates work there. With my luck I'd run into everybody under the sun if I chose either of those stores. The Quick Pick is small. But would they have a good variety of condoms? It's the kind of place you go if you need to pick up staples like milk, orange juice, toilet paper, and lottery tickets. I'm sure plenty of people consider condoms a staple.

After debating whether to travel to another town, I decide that is not worth the risk of me crashing the car, and head to the Quick Pick.

When I arrive, only five cars are in the lot, and none look familiar. Whew. I can do this.

With a deep breath, I unbuckle my seat belt and head inside.

I beeline for the toiletry area, searching the shelves, discovering a condom selection in the "family planning" aisle. Why is it called that? Shouldn't it be the anti-family planning aisle?

I look left and right to make sure I'm alone before I start shopping. The Quick Pick has plenty of latex condoms to choose from. There are also nonlatex condoms available for people who have a latex allergy. In class, Coach Woods said that a latex allergy is no excuse not to use a condom.

The store also has lambskin condoms, which I find creepy; plus, according to Coach Woods they don't protect against STDs. Not that I think Levi has an STD, but again—you always want to be prepared. Then there are condoms called "Ribbed for her pleasure." Just reading those words makes me blush. I blush even more furiously when I find a forty-condom variety box called the "Ecstasy Package."

They even have condoms with designs—there's plaid, polka dot, glow-in-the-dark, and more. I guess some women like decorated penises?

I snort at the idea of asking Levi, "Could you wear this camouflage condom please?"

Levi says he's normal-sized, but what if I insult him by getting the regular ones? I decide on a ten-pack of extra-large condoms that cost $7.20 because it seems like a better deal than only getting three for $2.50.

I grab some deodorant and a new toothbrush so I won't *only* be buying the condoms and head to the front of the store. A man is in line ahead of me, buying a bunch of lottery tickets. I check the time on my phone. It's taking longer than I'd like. Is he buying tickets for all his friends and family? I tap my toes on the floor.

"Tadpole?"

Oh. My. God.

I slowly turn around. It's Dad.

I should make a break for it. But that would be shoplifting and the last thing I need is to get arrested for stealing condoms. That kind of stuff stays on the Internet forever. USA Swimming probably wouldn't care to have a condom thief on the national team.

"Maggie? Are you okay?" Dad asks. "What are you doing here?"

Oh my god, oh my god. Most embarrassing moment ever.

I improvise, shaking the box of condoms. "Um, I had to pick these up for health class."

Dad sees what I'm holding. His face turns white, and his eyes balloon.

"We're using them on bananas," I add.

Dad's Adam's apple shifts as he swallows. "Uh, I figured the school would supply them…?" He scrubs a hand through his hair, eyes darting around the store. Is he scoping out the exits?

"Coach Woods said I need extra practice," I ramble. "I kept busting them in class."

"Well, good. Your mother and I have always been pleased at how seriously you take your schoolwork."

I hold up the box. "Do you think I got enough?"

Dad coughs into a fist. "Ten. Hm. Seems like you'll get plenty of practice. Extra-large, huh?"

I might die.

"Bananas are pretty big, you know." I clear my throat. "What are you doing here, Dad?"

He stares blankly. "Oh! We had a toothpick emergency."

"A toothpick emergency?"

"Yeah, we ran out of toothpicks for the hors d'oeuvres at the nursing home reception. So you came to buy the condoms yourself? Why didn't you put them on your mother's shopping list?"

"I couldn't put something like that on the list, Dad."

"Why not? It's just like any other school supply. You need pencils and paper, you put 'em on the list."

"Oh my god," I mumble.

"Next," the teller says, and I place my deodorant, toothbrush, and condoms on the counter.

Dad steps forward and adds his items to mine. "I'll pay for hers. My treat."

And that's when I die of mortification.

After swim practice at school one day, Levi gives me a ride. "Want to hang out at my house tonight?"

"I don't know why you're even asking," I reply. "We always go to your place."

"We can start going to your house when you start cleaning your room."

"Ugh, okay, Mom."

He chuckles.

"You're my best friend. That means you should love me, messes and all."

"I do love you, just not your messy room. I can't walk in there without stepping on something. I could twist an ankle." He points at me. "Coach would say going in your room is an unsanctioned activity."

"Levi," I warn, making him laugh again. "You really don't want to come over because of my room?"

"No, it's not that. Oma said she was making a Bundt cake today."

I grin widely at him. He is so cute. He's desperate to get home for a slice of his grandmother's cake.

At his place, however, he says we can't have cake until his laundry is in the wash. He's completely out of clean swimsuits and sweats, and unless I want him to wear dirty clothes tomorrow, he needs to start a load before doing anything else.

We go downstairs to the laundry room, where Levi unzips his athletic bag and shakes his swimsuits and sweats into the washing machine. He scoops detergent to pour on top of the clothes.

"Wait!" I cry as he dumps the detergent. "You're supposed to put the soap in first, then add the water, and *then* the clothes."

"Oh yeah?" Levi pulls out the nozzle to start the water, disregarding what I said.

"Levi! That's not how you do laundry."

He dips his mouth to my ear. "I'll show you how to do laundry."

With surprising ease he lifts me onto the washing machine and slips between my legs. Our faces at the same height, he begins to kiss my lips.

"What about your Bundt cake?" I whisper between kisses.

"Later. You taste sweeter." His hips grind against mine, totally turning me on. "You are so hot," he murmurs.

"Your lessons are paying off."

"You can't learn this," he says. His bangs fall into his eyes, and I brush them away, catching his blue gaze. Intense moments like this make me glad I picked up those condoms at the Quick Pick.

Footsteps clomp down the stairs. With a gasp, Levi pulls back from me right as Opa appears. I scramble down off the washer. When he sees us, his grandfather stops in his tracks.

"What are you doing in here, boy? Smooching?"

"No-no," Levi stutters. "Laundry."

Opa squints at us. "You got some mail."

"Where is it?" Levi asks.

Opa looks down at his empty hands and frowns. "I just had it. Oma! Where's the UPS package?"

Oma yells back down the stairs, "You left it in the kitchen! And it's a FedEx."

"That's what I said!" he hollers back.

"It doesn't matter," Levi groans.

Oma appears in the suddenly-crowded laundry room with a white box. "What are you kids doing in here?"

"Laundry," Levi and I say together.

His grandmother pats his cheek. "Come up for some cake when you're finished."

Oma disappears back upstairs with Opa at her heels, arguing over FedEx and UPS. Levi, meanwhile, lets out a long breath and rubs his eyes.

"Shit," I whisper. "Is Opa gonna tell anybody what we were doing?"

"Nah. By the time he gets upstairs he won't even remember because there's a hockey game on he wants to watch. But yeah, I hope he doesn't say anything."

My face heats. "Are you embarrassed by me?"

His eyes pop open. "Of course not. It would just complicate things. People wouldn't understand. They'd think I'm taking advantage of you."

"But you're not..." *It's the other way around.* "So what's in the box?"

Levi rips open the tab. Inside he finds a T-shirt and a crisp white envelope. He hands the shirt to me, freeing up both hands to open the envelope. I unfold the shirt. It says: *USA Junior National Team.*

"Holy crap!" I say. "Congrats!"

Levi reads aloud from the letter, "USA Swimming is pleased to inform you that you have been selected as a member of the United States Junior National Team."

I jump into his arms, crushing the letter to his chest, and he spins me around. I kiss him hard.

Abandoning the laundry and his box, Levi tugs me up the stairs. "What are we doing?"

"Going to your house to see if you got a box too," he replies. First we stop in the den to tell Oma and Opa. They smash Levi in a hug sandwich. Oma wipes tears from her eyes, proud that he's becoming a swim champion just like her.

"We'll have to celebrate," Opa says, patting Levi's back.

"Let's throw a party at the pizza place," Oma replies. She still looks at Levi as a little boy, but it's sweet.

Levi slips his hand into mine. "A joint party. Let's go see if you got a box."

On the drive to my house, Levi massages my thigh with a big smile on his face. But when we arrive and rush up to the front porch, there are no packages on the stoop. I check the mailbox to find a few catalogs and some bills, but nothing from USA Swimming.

"Maybe it came earlier and it's inside," Levi says, charging into the kitchen like he owns the place. But there's nothing there. Nothing except a note from Mom, telling me a pork chop is in the fridge. If a package came for me, Mom would've mentioned it or left it with the note about dinner.

"Your box'll come tomorrow," Levi says.

I shake my head. There's no way I got one. My times aren't there. I drag my feet on my starts. "Sometimes I feel like I am never going to be good enough."

He squeezes my shoulders. "Don't talk like that. You're great."

"Easy for you to say. You're already going to the trials."

"But you know that's not everything. I'm still nowhere near as good as I want to be—or need to be. I'm praying I don't bomb out in college."

"Why would that happen?"

"I'm fast, but not that fast."

"Levi."

"I think about it every night when I check the standings on the USA Swimming site. Yeah, I got a trial cut, but there are still fifty guys faster than me. Fifty! A few of them are three seconds faster than I am. Three seconds! I'm fast, but how the hell am I gonna make up three seconds? Will I ever be able to do it?"

I don't know, but at this point, I worry he has a much better chance than me.

~~

It's the weekend between regionals and state, so Levi and I have two practices on Saturday. During the time between them, we decide to check out Georgia's cheerleading competition in Nashville along with Hunter.

We enter the Vanderbilt gymnasium, where music is pounding and people are clapping, and it's like every cheerleader in the world has converged on this one spot. It's a pom-pom supernova.

"I've died and gone to heaven," Levi says.

"Why aren't there cheerleaders in baseball?" Hunter whines. That's always been his only complaint about his sport. I personally can't wait to see the routines. I love seeing roundoff back handsprings and flips, not to mention when the guy cheerleaders throw the girls in the air.

My guy friends walk a couple feet in front of me, waving at cheerleaders from other schools. Some give flirtatious smiles in return. I understand why; Hunter looks awfully good filling out his baseball uniform—jersey untucked, gray pants covered with red dirt, and Levi is in his athletic shorts, running tights, and that soft sweatshirt I want so bad. Last night after we made out in his bed, I put it on over my bra and underwear to tease him and told him I'm keeping it. He said I looked so sexy in it, he peeled it right back off me.

Now? I'm pretty sure other girls find it sexy on *him*.

One cheerleader wearing a tiny black and blue uniform that says *Ravens* bounces up in front of my friends. "Will you guys be cheering for me?"

"You think I could be a cheerleader?" Levi flirts.

Seeing him smile at another girl sets off firecrackers in my stomach. I'm surprised it hurts so much. Levi and I aren't together, and I've never cared in the past whether he's been interested in someone, but it seems I am now. I don't want to imagine him kissing a girl like he kissed me last night. He's not mine, but still.

I groan under my breath.

"What's wrong?" Hunter asks me.

"I'm hungry," I lie, because people believe it when I make that excuse.

"As soon as Levi's ready, we'll go to the concession stand." Hunter gestures at our friend, who is still talking to the Ravens cheerleader. "He seems to be doing okay today."

"Huh?"

"He's been acting weird. Shelby's cousin from Georgia is in town, and I asked him to go out with us tonight, but he said no. But he was interested when I showed him her picture a couple weeks ago."

Could that have something to do with me? "Really?"

"Yeah. Do you think he's depressed?"

"Depressed? What? No."

"Good. It makes absolutely no sense that he won't go out with Shelby's cousin for one night. She's smoking hot."

"He's fine," I grumble, imagining Levi on a date with another girl.

"Something's wrong with you too?"

"No, we're both *fine*."

Hunter turns to take in my face, blinking.

I pull a deep breath. What made me think I could keep my arrangement with Levi a secret forever? Hunter may not know the specifics, but he understands us well enough to know when something's off.

If he questions me again, I'll say I'm sad I didn't make the US Junior National Team, which is true. It devastated me, even though it was a long shot. Only twenty-five people nationwide made it. The only good news is that when I looked up the team online, Roxy didn't make it either. I grin evilly to myself.

The concession stand only has greasy pizza and cotton candy, which won't help me at practice later, so Levi pulls a protein bar from his backpack to tide me over.

I take a seat between Levi and Hunter in the stands near the Hundred Oaks basketball and football teams. I love that all these guys came out to support the cheerleading squad. Levi's thigh touches mine, but he makes no move to put space between us, even when Noah Thompson, a basketball player I've always been friendly with—but Levi can't stand—turns around to talk to me.

"Did you see the new Bond movie?" Noah asks.

I shake my head.

"Oh my God, you have to see it. First, Bond free jumps from a satellite in orbit above the earth and lands in the middle of Siberia. Then he stows away on a train into North Korea! Then he steals a nuke from the North Koreans! Then he does it with this lady from North Korea on the back of an ATV!"

"What, you gonna tell her the whole movie?" Levi asks.

"I'd rather she just go see it with me." Noah gives me a not-so-subtle look.

"She doesn't like action movies," Levi replies, rolling his eyes.

"What crawled up your ass, Lucassen?" Noah snaps.

Lucky for me Hundred Oaks is cheering next, distracting the guys from their pissing contest. When Georgia runs out onto the gym floor, Levi and Hunter jump to their feet, pumping their arms in the air.

"Woooo! Georgia! Woooo!" Hunter yells.

"Georgia!" I scream, clapping.

Levi wolf-whistles.

Our cheerleaders wave at our section and hop up and down. Dance music blasts from the speakers.

The football and basketball players go nuts, holding up posters they made. Several football players—seven to be exact—rip off their shirts to reveal they've painted their chests. Together they spell 100 OAKS.

"Ready, okay!" the cheerleaders yell in unison, clapping once.

The routine starts with Georgia nailing a roundoff followed by three back handsprings and a back tuck. I spot David Cantor sitting a few rows away, cheering for Georgia. I nudge Levi and Hunter, pointing him out. Levi smiles a little because David is here; Hunter is wide-eyed.

The cheerleaders fan out across the stage, doing splits and jumps and all sorts of other tricks that do not seem physically possible.

When Georgia does a split, Noah turns around again. "The North Korean lady did the splits with James Bond in bed."

Levi flicks him in the forehead.

It's really fun, dancing along with the cheerleaders and the loud, rhythmic music. Levi puts an arm around my waist, pulling me closer, sliding his hand up and down my hip. My mind flashes to last night, when he took off every scrap of my clothing and rocked against me in his boxers. Is Levi thinking of it too? Oh my God, are we naughty dancing?

Hunter happens to look over and see this, and I quickly step away from Levi. Hunter's mouth falls open.

The routine ends and we scream for Georgia.

When we sit back down, Levi's thigh touches mine as he leans over and says quietly in my ear, "You were making me hot."

"Like sweaty hot?" I joke.

"No, like *I want to take you under the bleachers* hot."

My whole body is overcome by heat. I completely understand how he gets girls into closets so quickly. It's that voice. Or is it because he's like a Dutch sex god? Anyway, it's difficult not to take him up on the offer.

Hunter dips his head to speak with me. "I think I know why Levi's not interested in Shelby's cousin anymore. It's because he wants to take *you* under the bleachers."

"It's not polite to eavesdrop." I lightly punch him in the thigh and expect him to make a joke, but he just sits there gripping his knees.

While waiting to see who won the competition, we collect Georgia and go hang out in the lobby. When we arrived at Vanderbilt, sun streaked through the floor-to-ceiling windows. Now it's starting to rain outside; water drips down the glass.

I tell Georgia she did great, and she beams. Their performance made everybody from our school hyper—the football and basketball guys surround the cheerleaders, hugging them and hollering.

Noah Thompson sees Levi giving Georgia a big hug and calls over at us, "Levi Lucassen rocks my world!" and Levi flips him off.

I bend down to hug her too. Hunter stands there, not smiling. Georgia nudges his side. "Hey, what's wrong?"

"Does Georgia know something's going on between you guys?" Hunter asks me and Levi.

Georgia's eyes grow huge as she glances between us. She jumps and claps as if doing one of her routines. "I knew you guys would get together one day!"

She did? Levi and I just look at each other. At one time I think we would've cracked up, but not now.

"We're not together," Levi says.

Hunter crosses his arms. "But you're fooling around?"

"Who said anything about that?" I ask.

"I'm not blind. I can tell something's going on with you guys. And somebody's going to get hurt."

"Nahhh," Levi says, avoiding eye contact with Hunter.

"I like Shelby a lot more than she likes me. I can tell you it hurts." His head droops, and Georgia places a hand on his arm. I knew what was happening with Shelby bothered him, but not this much.

"I've been telling you," Georgia starts, "You didn't set limits on your relationship with Shelby. You should've said you wanted a relationship before you slept with her. By hooking up without the commitment, you set your own value short. She gets to be casual without having to be your girlfriend."

Hunter gives Georgia a hard stare. That was harsh, but friends should be straight with each other, and she's not wrong. Giving without agreement sets you up for heartbreak.

Right then, David appears beside our group, pushing his glasses up on his nose. "You did great," he tells Georgia, wrapping an arm around her for a side hug.

Levi gives David one of his guy handshakes and Hunter nods at him, but keeps a close watch on Georgia and David as they talk and smile at each other.

"Why are you acting like a dad all of a sudden?" I ask Hunter.

"If he hurts her," Hunter mutters to me, "I'm going to rip out his spine."

"Down, boy," I tease. I can understand why Hunter's so protective. When that douchebag linebacker Kevin cheated on Georgia, Hunter spent a lot of time comforting her. Their friendship is a lot like mine and Levi's. Or at least, the way ours used to be.

After watching the cheerleading squad win the second place trophy, Levi and I go to our second practice of the day, but it's hard to get Hunter out of my head. He was still acting pretty reserved when we left. Hooking up with Levi is risky, but I had no idea it might upset one of our friends. Plus, seeing Levi smile at the Ravens cheerleader felt crappy. All these thoughts and feelings distract me, making me sluggish in the pool.

Coach chides me from the deck. "Let's pick it up, Maggie! Pick it up!"

I swim faster, but my heart isn't all the way there. Between laps when I'm out of breath, clinging to the side of the pool, Levi glides up next to me and nudges my side. "You okay?"

My nod back is a lie.

It's still raining after practice. As we're leaving the Sportsplex, Levi opens an umbrella and holds it above our heads as we hurry to his truck. I let out a sigh of relief once we're inside, dry and warm. Rain pelts the windshield, punctuating the silence between me and my best friend.

On the way home in the pouring rain, Levi peers over at me from the driver's seat.

"I'm not hurting you, am I?" he asks.

"What?"

"You heard what Hunter said. He's worried we're going to get hurt."

I was pretty jealous when he talked to that other girl earlier, but if I tell him that, it could make things awkward between us, and that's the last thing I need. I want us to stay normal.

The windshield wipers are on high, going as fast as they go. Still, it's tough to see through the storm.

"Everything's good," I say. "Hunter's overreacting because of Shelby."

"Yeah. You're right." Levi taps his fingers on the steering wheel. "I shouldn't have said that about going under the bleachers."

"How could you know Hunter has superhuman hearing? I mean, I barely heard you."

We listen to a couple of songs on the radio, and I stare out the window at rainy, gray skies until he speaks again. "Maybe we should cool it from now on."

I twist to look at him. He's chewing on his lower lip. I didn't like him talking to that girl today, but it's not like I'm in love with him. I enjoy being with my friend, hanging out, talking, and kissing. I really like the kissing. But is that because I like kissing? Or because I like *him*? Do they go hand in hand? I try to imagine myself kissing Hunter like we did a couple years ago in truth or dare. It does not entice me at all.

I lean my head against the window.

"Magpie?" he says.

The last thing I want is to scare off my best friend. I told him this wouldn't get weird.

"Yeah, that's fine," I say a little louder than I would have liked. "Thanks for the lessons. They were illuminating."

He grins. "You're welcome. Now you can hook up with Noah the basketball ignoramus."

"I think it's you he wants. Remember earlier? *Levi Lucassen rocks my world!*" I mimic, and we crack up until he drops me off at my house.

I go inside, hang my jacket in the foyer, and head into the kitchen where I find a note from Mom saying she and Dad won't be back until after the sixteenth birthday party they're catering. She left me some lasagna to heat up, but I'm not hungry.

I climb the stairs to my room and sit down on my bed. From my nightstand, I pick up the picture of Levi and me that Dad took at the Speedo Classic in Daytona last year. Our arms are wrapped around each other and we're smiling like we've won the Olympics. I run my fingers over his happy face, then place the photo back in its spot and lie down on my bed.

See? I knew this would be fine. We hooked up and now we're done. I know what an orgasm feels like now; I bet I could even give myself one. I have more experience.

Nobody got hurt.

So why do I feel like crawling under the covers and not coming out?

Wildflowers

Later that night I'm forced out from under the covers because Georgia texts me, saying she's coming over.

When I let her in my house, the skin under her eyes is puffy and pink.

I give her a hug. "You okay?"

"My mom was being terrible, as usual. She pointed out everything I did wrong in my routine today."

"You did great! And the team came in second. That's all that matters, right?"

"Not to Mom. I didn't smile enough apparently."

"I saw your whole performance and you were totally smiling."

Georgia shuts her eyes. "I don't know how to make my mom happy so she'll leave me alone."

It's hard to relate because my parents aren't controlling at all. They want whatever I want, and I want to swim. I can't imagine doing it because someone else demanded it of me, like how Jason's father gets pissed when he comes in second, or the way Georgia's mom critiques her every move when it comes to cheerleading.

"You love cheering, right?" I ask.

"More than anything."

"Then doing your best and having a good time is all that matters."

"It sucks having to listen to Mom tell me I'm not good enough."

"You should tell her that."

Georgia makes a guffawing noise. "As if she listens to a word I say."

I don't know how to respond. "We need ice cream."

"Oh my god, yes. I'm starving. Mom's still on the no-sugar diet."

Georgia helps me raid our fridge and then we climb the stairs to my room. There, I kick the clothes littering the floor out of our way, and move my gym bag, clearing a spot for her on my bed. Once we're settled and listening to music, she doesn't beat around the bush.

"What's going on with you and Leaves?" she asks through a mouthful of chocolate chip cookie dough.

I wrap my arms around my shins and prop my chin on my knee.

"You can talk to me."

"I know."

"So go ahead. 'Levi and I...'" she starts.

I take a deep breath. "Levi and I... I asked him to teach me how to fool around."

Her eyebrows shoot up toward the ceiling. "You just came right out and asked him that?"

"Yup."

"And he said yeah?"

"We talked about it first, but eventually, yeah, he said yes."

"That takes courage… How long have you been doing this?"

"A few weeks."

She squeals. "Are you guys dating?"

"No."

"And you're okay with that?" Georgia cocks her head. "Don't you want more?"

Am I supposed to want more? I don't know if I do. Why does my relationship with Levi have to be one thing or another? The way Georgia is questioning me, it's like I'm doing something bad. But it's my body, my life, my needs. And I've been happy.

"I like what I had going with Levi."

"Had?"

"Today after Hunter found out, Levi said we should probably stop."

"That stinks." Sighing, Georgia scoops a big bite of ice cream into her mouth.

"Hunter's probably right. One of us will end up hurt." *And I'm afraid it might be me.*

"Seriously though. How was it?"

I smile, remembering what it's like to curl up with Levi. He makes me feel fun, sexy, and wanted all at once.

"It was great," I tell her, and she squeals again, wanting to know all the details. I give her a few—he's a great kisser and knows what he's doing with his hands—but the memories feel special, and I want to wrap them up in tissue paper and hide them deep in the memory box in my closet.

She glances at me tentatively. "So you think it's okay to experiment with a guy and not date him?"

"It was working okay for us…and it felt amazing."

"God, my mom would kill me if I did that. And could you imagine what the people at church would say? I don't understand how Hunter and Shelby have been doing the casual thing either. I guess I never figured it was an option for girls."

I get what she's saying. There's definitely a double standard. It seems guys can do whatever they want sexually *because boys will be boys*. But girls have every right to experiment too. Can't girls be girls?

I scoop a bite of ice cream. "I think you can experiment. But you both have to be on the same page, or I bet somebody will get hurt."

"So you and Leaves aren't going to hook up anymore?" Her forehead crinkles.

"I guess not."

"But think of all the cute, future Olympian babies you'd have!" My mouth falls open.

Georgia rambles, "I've always thought you guys were perfect for each other but that you weren't ready yet. Like, you needed to grow a little more."

She's not wrong. I think I could definitely come to feel more for him. I mean, I already love him as a friend, but maybe I like him more than that. But there's no guarantee he would feel the same.

One time at Junior Nationals, I swam against Deanna Rodriguez, a fifteen-year-old who had made the overall US National Team. Right before the start, I questioned whether I should even bother swimming the race, because there was a high probability I would lose. What did I do?

I dove in.

If I were to look deep inside myself and figure out I want more with Levi, I would tell him. But do I?

When Georgia goes home later that night, I swipe on my phone to text Levi.

Good night, I type.

Immediately he writes back **Good night M.**

<hr />

Monday morning while waiting for music appreciation class to start, Hunter and I are messing around like we're back in elementary school.

Hunter plays "Twinkle, Twinkle" on the xylophone, and I'm going to town on the triangle. Our music teacher dresses like a hippie who never left Woodstock and wants us to become *one with ourselves*, whatever that means, so generally we spend most of class listening to different kinds of music and describing how it makes us feel.

"Your song makes me feel like shit," Levi calls from across the room, and Hunter and I start playing louder and louder. Other kids groan at how bad we are.

"Hey, listen," Hunter says. "I'm sorry if I upset you the other day."

Ding, ding, ding, I play on the triangle. I don't think anyone can hear us talking thanks to our horrible music. "It's all right."

"No, it's not. I'm wrecked about Shelby and took it out on you and Levi. Did I mess things up for you guys?"

"I don't know," I say honestly. "At first I didn't think it would be hard to stop, but now I'm not sure how I feel about him."

"Do you think about him when you wake up in the morning?"

"Well, *yeah*. He's my ride to practice."

Hunter gives me a look. "You know what I mean."

"Yeah, I think about him a lot."

"That probably means something."

It *could* mean something, but it might not. I never had romantic feelings for Levi before we started kissing. What if fooling around with Levi is fueling stronger romantic emotions that may or may not be real? Once it happened, feelings started blooming, as if I threw a bunch of seeds over my shoulder, and a month later, wildflowers were all over my yard. They are beautiful, but not what I had planned. Is that okay? Or will it all grow out of control and mess up our carefully tended friendship? I'm not sure if I ever wanted to tend a garden to begin with. Have the romantic feelings taken over my ability to think rationally?

Not to mention the other emotions that came along with making out: jealousy, when I think of Levi with another girl; insecurity, when I worry I'm asking too much of him and could be negatively affecting our friendship. Are we even *Maggie and Levi* anymore?

One of my classmates smashes the cymbals together, jerking me from my thoughts.

The music teacher, Mrs. McKean, sails into the room, wearing a long flowing dress and no joke—a turban. I wouldn't be surprised if she pulls out a crystal ball and tries to tell our fortunes.

She smiles at Hunter and me. "Beautiful song, my friends. You truly belong among the stars that twinkle."

Levi shakes his head at us. I go sit in the chair next to him and smile cheekily. "Did you hear that? I truly belong among the stars."

He smiles, but it looks a little pained. I want to ask him if he's doing okay, but I don't want to seem overbearing either. That's another thing that sucks about this murky area between friendship and something more. I question everything I do and say, rather than just act like myself. It's hard to know who I am with him anymore.

Tuesday morning, I find out what was wrong with Levi. He texted he's not swimming today. What? He hasn't missed a day since he sprained his arm in third grade.

His message says: I have a cold.

That is not good. The state championship is in four days!

Feel better, I tell him.

I change into my suit, throw on my sweats, and jog downstairs. Dad is standing there still half asleep as usual, holding my snack bag.

"Dad, Levi can't go this morning. Can you drive me?"

He gives me a sympathetic look. "Your mom and I have an early pitch session with the mayor's office about the pajama party, and I need to review our presentation a couple more times."

"But I've never driven all the way to Nashville," I complain.

"Traffic will be light this time of day, and you can take the back roads. You'll be fine."

Jingling my keys, I take a deep breath, climb into the car, and start driving. I make it to the Sportsplex okay, but I'm ten minutes late because I couldn't bring myself to go over forty miles per hour.

"You're late," Coach Josh says, obnoxiously checking his watch.

"Dad made me drive again," I say, and Coach makes an O with his mouth. That's the last I hear out of him because he knows driving is punishment enough for me.

School is a little lonely without Levi. I eat lunch with Hunter and Shelby, as well as Georgia, who spends most of the time turned around in her chair, flirting with David who's sitting at another table. Hunter and Shelby are arguing under their breath right in front of me. I can totally hear everything.

"I don't see why you won't come to my cousin's wedding with me," Shelby says.

"Because," Hunter replies, "you know people will ask if I'm your boyfriend."

"So what?"

"Clearly we're together. If people don't think I'm your boyfriend, they'll assume I'm your boy toy or that I'm using you or something."

"No, they won't."

"Well that's how I feel. I'm not going unless we make this relationship real already."

Pain flits across Shelby's face. "I'm sick of fighting with you."

"Me, too. Just go out with me."

"Hunt, I've told you, I'm scared. I can't handle long distance. Let's keep this casual."

"If we're casual, there's no reason for me to go with you to a family wedding."

Awkward. I want to smush their heads together and make them kiss and tell them to stop their foolishness. Yeah, he's going away in three months, but that doesn't mean they can't be together.

I decide to text Levi: School without you is pure torture

He writes back: I miss you too. x

I stare down at my phone. Is that little *x* a kiss? The other day he said we can't hook up anymore, but now he's texting me kisses? Has the sickness ravaged his brain? Maybe it's a typo. I nod to myself. Typo. Totally.

The day gets even weirder when Noah, the basketball player Levi doesn't like, waits for me outside calculus class.

"Did you understand any of that about infinity limits?" he asks.

"Not a bit."

He walks me down the hall. "You seem different, Maggie."

"Different how?"

"Relaxed and happy. To be honest, you're kind of a hard girl to get to know."

"Really?" I've always tried to be nice to people.

Noah scratches the top of his head, peeking at me sideways. "I mean, Levi's around all the time, and that's kind of intimidating... Plus you're so serious and focused."

"I kind of have to be. Swimming is my life."

"Whatever you're doing different, I like it." He winks and takes off down the hall toward a group of basketball players carrying on about a pick-up game after school.

By the time afternoon swim practice is over, I'm feeling more confident in my driving abilities, so I stop by Foothills Diner to get some soup for Levi. When I get to his house, Oma greets me at the door. She grabs Pepper's collar as the dog sniffs the paper bag containing chicken soup and warm bread.

"How is he?" I ask Oma.

She gives me a knowing smile. "Behaving like any other sick man—acting like it's the end of the world."

I climb the stairs to his room. Without knocking I go in and find him watching a dirt bike race on TV. His bed is covered in tissues. A book called *The Raven Boys* is sitting on his quilt. He's wearing a hoodie and mesh shorts, and thick socks cover his feet.

When he sees me, he drags himself to an upright position. "Hey."

"Don't overdo it," I say, moving to sit next to him. I push him forward so I can fluff the pillow behind his head. "I brought you soup."

"Between you and Oma, my blood is gonna be made of soup."

"You're welcome."

He smiles a little and coughs. The skin around his nose is red.

"Will you be able to swim on Saturday?" I ask.

"Nothing's keeping me out of that pool." He coughs again.

Seeing him like this, all flushed and sad and worn out, I can't help but cradle his cheek and kiss his forehead. When I pull away, he gives me a funny look.

"Don't get too close," he says. "You might catch whatever I've got."

"I never get sick. I'll risk it."

Levi points at a bottle of antibacterial gel on the nightstand. "At least use some of that. It's Oma's."

After lathering up my hands, I open the plastic soup container and pass it to him. He practically inhales the broth.

"You want to watch a movie or something?" I ask, taking the empty plastic container and setting it next to his pile of Harry Potters.

"I'm actually kinda tired." He lies back down and pulls the covers up around his waist, then pats my knee. "Do you want to stay for a little bit? Tell me about your day?"

I go around to the other side of the bed, sweeping his tissues aside, and crawl in, but stay on top of the covers to avoid germs—karma could catch up with me. I lather up with the hand gel again, cozy up next to him, and rest a hand on his chest. He cradles my hand in his and shuts his eyes. With my other hand, I play with his hair. It's gotten so long it nearly reaches his chin. Pretty soon he'll look like Pepper.

"You should let me put little braids in your hair," I tease.

"I'd look stupid."

"You'd look sexy. My sexy shark."

He shifts under my hand on his chest. "Don't turn me on." He laughs, but it turns into another cough. "I'm ill."

"I figured a guy wouldn't let a little cold get in the way of sexy times."

"You're right. I must be dying."

"You're not dying."

"Lesson number three: Guys always want it. Except for when they are dying."

We lie curled up together talking until his mom comes home earlier than usual. She appears in the doorway, dressed in a black power suit and red skyscraper high heels, carrying a tray with a bowl and a book.

I pull my hand out from under his and sit up, smoothing my hair. Ms. Lucassen considers me for a long moment. She's found us lounging on his bed listening to music and hanging out before, but never holding hands.

Levi's eyes flutter open, and he says hi to his mom, who fusses over him like I did, feeling the temperature of his forehead and fluffing his blankets.

"I brought you some soup and the next book in that Raven series you're reading," she says, and he moans, "Not more soup," but immediately digs into it.

"I should go," I say, getting to my feet. "I still need to do homework."

"See you Saturday at the meet," Ms. Lucassen says.

Outside his room, I start down the stairs, but remember I left my gloves on his dresser. I am heading back up when I hear them talking.

"Is something going on with you and Maggie?" his mom asks.

"No."

"Are you sure about that?"

How do moms always know?

"I care about her," he says slowly.

"You both have a lot going on with swimming right now," Ms. Lucassen replies. "I don't want things to get complicated for you. You have trials in a few months."

"Right. There's nothing going on."

I grab the staircase railing to hold myself up. He said nothing's going on between us. As if these past few weeks of growing closer physically have meant nothing. His words feel like drowning.

But would I say anything different?

Swimcest

It takes Levi a few days to get over his cold, but by the time he picks me up for the pool on Friday morning, he seems much better. I missed him a lot this week. Not being able to see him for months when I'm at college this fall will be miserable. I don't want to think about it.

"Are you going to swim this morning?" I ask.

"I think I'll stretch and get in a quick workout, but not do too much. Are you feeling okay? I'm worried I might've gotten you sick."

"I'm fine."

He looks over at me from behind the wheel. "You nervous about state?"

"I got this."

A smile appears on his face. "Yeah, you do." He reaches over to pat my knee, and I squeeze his hand. I find myself tracing his fingers, wanting to kiss them. Wanting them on my body. I bring his hand to my mouth and kiss his knuckles.

"God, I wish we didn't have practice," I whisper.

He fidgets in the driver's seat. "I thought we agreed we can't do this anymore."

"We did…but that hasn't stopped me from wanting it." *From wanting you.*

Levi pulls into the parking lot, throws the car into park, and pulls me into his arms. He's always grumpy in the morning, but it turns out he can be turned on too. I might drown in his kisses. My fingers slip under his shirt to touch his warm, velvety skin, and soon we're both having trouble breathing. I love the noises he's making as we fog up the windows. He eases me onto my back, deliciously teasing my throat with his lips.

"God, I want you," he murmurs.

Right as things are heating up, someone pounds on the window, and we break apart. I peer through the fogged-up glass at Coach Josh while Levi adjusts his warm up pants to cover his excitement.

"You're late again," Coach says.

"Shit," we say together.

Coach shakes his head. "Move it."

My mouth falls open as Coach stalks toward the Sportsplex doors. "Shit, shit, shit."

Before Levi will let me out of the truck, he hugs me long and hard. "We weren't doing anything wrong, okay?"

"Except *swimcest*."

We laugh awkwardly, touching our foreheads together. I hold

on to him as we try to catch our breath. I can't remember ever feeling so good. But it's also like I just pulled up to a train crossing, with flashing red barriers dropping and warning bells dinging. Will the train smash into me or pass me by?

When we head inside to the pool, Coach puts us straight to work on stretching and studying today's workout on the whiteboard. We've been tapering all week, so it's only 3,000 yards today. Pretty easy.

What's not so easy? As soon as laps are over, Coach wants to see us privately. With a dark-green beach towel tied around his waist, Levi walks ahead of me off the pool deck, pulling off his swim cap and shaking out his hair like Pepper emerging from Normandy Lake. I hike my towel up around my chest and go change my clothes. The entire time I'm shaking. Levi's already in Coach's office by the time I arrive.

"Are you out of your minds?" Coach blurts.

Levi and I glance at each other.

"Um, no?" I say.

"Yup, you're out of your damned minds," Coach decides. "Maggie, if you get your cuts in Huntsville in a couple weeks, you both will be going to the *United States Olympic trials*, but instead of practicing, you're messing around in Levi's truck."

"It's my fault," I say.

"*Yours?*"

"I started it."

"*You?*"

Coach takes off his visor, runs a hand through his hair, and puts his visor back on. This guy knows us as well as our parents do—if not better. Hell, he knows when it's my time of the month, because I always get a little sluggish in the water. So I guess he thinks this is a little out of character for me, and he would be right.

"You two are best friends," Coach says. "Teammates. This could get awkward. You saw how Susannah dating Lucas affected her times last year. I don't want that happening to you two."

"It won't," Levi and I rush to say.

"Look, I can't control what you two do out of the pool, but it better not affect your performance here, understand?"

"Yes, Coach," I say.

"Yes, sir," Levi says with a nod.

"And I better not see what I saw this morning in your truck again."

We file out of his office. I barely have the energy to cross the parking lot. I'm so humiliated and disappointed I upset my coach. God, he calls my mother when I have a bad headache. What if he calls her about this?

By the time Levi and I get to school, we've missed first period. Barely a word has been spoken since Coach chewed us out.

Levi starts to open his truck door but I say, "Wait. Can we talk?"

He clears his throat. "Sure."

"I'm confused." I can barely hear myself say it.

He reaches over to my side of the truck, gently taking my hand. "What are you confused about?"

"I don't want to stop, but I know we should, but I can't imagine not being with you. Both as a friend, and maybe something more. But I don't know. I just know I'm scared…and I really want to kiss you some more."

He chuckles softly, sadly. Then rolls his shoulders. "Things are intense with us."

"They are?"

"You don't feel it?"

"It's not like this with other girls?"

He shakes his head. "Not even close."

Maybe I didn't recognize the spark because I've never been with another guy—well, except for the juicy steak dinner guy at Cal. Sure, I think of Levi all the time, but I figured it's because the kissing is great.

"Maybe it's because we're friends," I say.

He gazes over at me. "I didn't expect to feel this way."

Oh my God. Is he telling me he has feelings for me? Hearing that is like hitting the beach and rushing for the sparkling blue water.

"But it's already affecting both of us in the pool," he goes on. "*I'm training for the Olympic trials…* I've been working toward that my entire life. And I dunno, maybe I'll do amazing and get on the team. After that, there's college, and who knows what might happen then." His voice fades. It sounds like he's breaking inside. "I'm not sure I have room for a girlfriend."

I know what he's saying. Or, at least I think I do. I haven't been sure of anything the past few days.

He hops out of the truck and starts walking toward the school. I follow him. We reach the school entrance and he holds the glass door open for me.

"So what are you saying?" I ask. "That we can't do this anymore, but you have feelings? There has to be some way we can have swimming and *us*."

"I'm not sure if I *want* a relationship," Levi says under his breath. "All I said was that the feelings are intense with us."

I really don't understand what he's saying. But on the other hand, I don't understand how I feel either.

"Let's get through the state championship tomorrow," I say, "And then we can talk."

"We should get to class." He turns around, throwing his bag over his shoulder, and heads down the hall.

I guess that conversation is over.

That night at Jiffy Burger, things are still off.

It's not the fries. Those are perfect as ever. At least, they taste the same—salty and piping hot. I'm just not enjoying them as much as I normally do.

It started before we even arrived at the diner when Levi texted to say he was running late and couldn't pick me up. Mom drove me here before she went to work, which was awkward.

"Coach Josh called," she said. "He said you seemed stressed at practice, and he's worried. He thought maybe we should talk."

My coach is such a meddler. At least he didn't seem to tell her about me and Levi making out.

"Is something going on?" she asked.

"No."

"He mentioned Levi seemed stressed too. Are you guys fighting?"

My seat belt felt tighter than usual. "No, why would you think that?"

She glanced over from the driver's seat. "Because you two were acting weird when your dad and I came home last week."

I shrugged, trying to act nonchalant. "I don't know what Coach is talking about. I'm nervous about state tomorrow, I guess."

"You know you can talk to me if you need to," Mom said. We're both quiet for a moment, and I'm grateful when she changes the subject. "Did I tell you about our new clients? This couple wants a *Game of Thrones*–themed wedding…because nothing says love like murder."

By the time I got to Jiffy Burger, Levi was already seated in our booth. I thought he couldn't drive me because he was behind schedule. Was he really running late? He's never lied to me before…

I shove a bunch of fries in my mouth, totally stress eating.

"Are you excited for tomorrow?" Hunter asks us.

Levi and I nod.

"Oh, Maggie," Georgia starts. "Get this. Noah Thompson asked me if you have a prom date."

Levi's chin jerks up.

Hunter looks back and forth at the two of us.

"Really?" I ask, continuing to fork salad into my mouth.

"I told him you might be going with Levi."

Levi's eyes won't meet mine.

I set my fork down and finish chewing. "I doubt I can go to prom. It's the same day as the Spring Spotlight in Cincinnati."

May 14. It's two months from now. That's my final chance to qualify for the trials. Even if I get my cuts in Huntsville or Atlanta prior to that race, I will still need the practice in a long course meet. I have to go no matter what. Early that day I'll have prelims, and then hopefully I'll be in the finals that afternoon. Depending on how I do, I'll either be celebrating that night, completely exhausted, or crying my eyes out. Prom isn't really on my mind.

Okay. That's a lie. It kind of is.

I would love to go to my senior prom. I'd love to go shopping with my mom and Georgia for a dress and get my hair and makeup done. But Cincinnati is four hours away. As it stands now, to make the prom on time, I'd probably be racing from the pool with damp hair, smelling of chlorine.

I smile to myself at the idea of dancing with Levi surrounded by twinkling lights as I stare up into his glimmering blue eyes. Even if we could only make it in time for one dance at the very end of the night, it'd be worth it.

"Yeah, prom's out for me," Levi says, digging into his burger like the dance is no big deal. "Unless, like, I tweet at Missy Franklin, ask her to be my date, and she says yes. Then I'd go."

Georgia bites her lip.

I suck in a deep breath, and fake laugh at his joke. I don't care if the hottest guy on earth invited me to prom, I'd say no. I wouldn't want to hurt Levi.

When we're leaving, I whisper to Levi, "I'm not interested in Noah. Just in case you were wondering."

He nods once. "I'll see you tomorrow morning. Pick you up at eight." He walks across the parking lot, jingling his keys.

It's not until he's getting in his truck that I realize, for the first time ever, he didn't offer me a ride home.

∼⌒∼

The state championship is taking place in Nashville at the Vanderbilt University pool.

As promised, Levi picks me up in the morning, grumpy as ever. Our parents will meet us there a bit later because we need time to warm up and get in the zone. Even though he said me he would, it surprises me when Levi picks me up considering I had to bum a ride from Hunter last night. It pissed me off, to be honest.

On top of that, I'm so nervous about going up against Roxy today, I can't sit still in the truck. "I'm starting to understand why you hook up at meets."

"Huh?" Levi replies.

"I'm antsy about seeing Roxy. I wish I could get my mind off it."

My friend grunts and doesn't say anything. My face flushes when I realize it sounds like I was asking him to fool around. God, what is wrong with me? The past day has been stressful enough for us. He's been acting weird ever since I said we should talk after state is over. I'm probably making things worse.

But it's true. When the meet is over, maybe tomorrow or the next day, I do want to talk to Levi about our feelings. He said things are intense with us, and I agree. A vision of him on top of me flits into my head.

I shift in my seat again.

I would feel a lot better about today if I had some assurances of how things will go with Levi.

"We're going to talk after the meet, right?" I ask.

He drums his hands on the steering wheel, sneaking a look my way. "Okay, whatever."

At the pool, Coach Josh claps us both on the back when he sees us.

"Feeling good?" he asks.

My stomach feels like piranhas are swimming around inside me. "Yeah," I lie.

Coach raises an eyebrow. He doesn't believe me for a second.

I stow my bag in a locker and head to the practice lanes, where I meet up with Coach again, who's talking to Levi, Jason, and Susannah. Jason and Susannah go to private school and have other swim coaches here, but like me, they depend on Coach Josh.

When I hop down into the first practice lane, that's when I see her. Roxy. She's in the next lane over. I take a deep breath. I can do this. I may not have as many Twitter followers as she does, but I'm faster than her in the pool. I know it.

I wave at Roxy, and she ignores me. That's fine. I'm taking care of myself right now. Like Coach said, I'm concentrating on me, my body, my race. This is my day. *I will win 200 back.*

Prelims go okay. In 200 free, I score the best time of any swimmer in any of the heats, which is amazing. Normally I am very focused on time and how I can shave off five-tenths of a second so I can qualify for the trials but not today. The state championships aren't about times. They're about the win. And I want it bad.

For the 200 back heat though, my time is a hundredth of a second slower than Roxy's and one other swimmer. I can make that up in the race. I know I can. Without another glance at her, I hop out of the pool.

I spend the morning cheering for kids from Hundred Oaks and New Wave during their races. Levi keeps his distance, which hurts, but I understand why. Our minds should be on the pool. I can't help but sneak glances his way, and he keeps catching me. He shifts uncomfortably in his seat.

Later in the afternoon when it's time for the 200 back final, I go into the locker room, take a shower to warm up, and pull my sweats on over my suit. I picture my start, thinking hard about making sure my feet don't drag across the water. I breathe deeply as I put my tennis shoes back on for the walk across the pool deck.

When I go back into the hallway, I find Levi talking to Roxy. She's very close to him. Smiling. Looking at his lips. She touches his hip. He doesn't stop her. Another minute and she could have him under the bleachers.

My goggles fall from my hand to the floor.

Roxy looks away from Levi and gives me a taunting smile. "Oh, hey, Maggie. Levi and I were just catching up."

I can't help but cover my mouth and let out a little cry. When he sees my reaction, Levi's face starts turning red. I walk up to him, grab his arm, and pull him away from her.

"Territorial, much?" she snaps.

Once we're in a private corner, I lay into him. "What the hell?"

He looks past me over my shoulder. "What?"

"How could you do that right in front of me?"

"I didn't do anything."

"You let Roxy touch your hip."

185

His voice turns more gentle. "I wouldn't fool around with her, Mags. You know that."

"Oh." I breathe deeply through my nose, trying to calm down. "I don't see why you'd be around another girl anyway."

"It's not like you and I are dating."

That's true. I basically encouraged him a couple weeks ago to have sex with another girl if he needed to. But I would never suggest he hook up with my rival! Especially not in a place I might see him…

"Why would you do that right outside my locker room?" I snap, and pause, suddenly understanding. "Did you want me to see you with her?"

"It wasn't about Roxy," he says, shutting his eyes. "It could've been any girl."

"Any girl?"

"I told you, Mags. I don't think I want a girlfriend right now. I *can't*."

"So you *were* hoping to hook up with somebody else?"

He doesn't respond, and I know I'm right.

The announcement for the next race—200 back—my race—says it's about to start and swimmers should get ready to take their marks. I cover my eyes with my hands. A sob falls from my mouth.

When he sees how upset I am, Levi takes my elbow. "I'm sorry. I got scared."

"Scared of what?" My voice breaks.

"That we're getting too close."

My lips tremble. *Don't cry, don't cry.* "So rather than talk to me you decide to piss me off, hurt my feelings"—*break my heart*—"right before my race? Right before the *fucking* state championship? Couldn't you have kept it in your pants until after? Real mature, asshole."

Not waiting for him to respond, I turn and march toward the pool, ready to win this race. But the moment I hit the deck, Roxy looks over at me and waves with a smirk. The air whooshes out of me.

I walk up to the water, splash some on my hands. Make sure my suit is in place.

"Maggie."

Levi is behind me now. I ignore him.

"Magpie."

"Don't," I say through gritted teeth.

"I was wrong. I'm so sorry. So sorry." His frantic expression mirrors the time Pepper ran away with her leash in the woods by Normandy Lake and we couldn't find her anywhere. "You got this race."

"Go. Away."

His eyebrows pinch together. "Let's talk after."

"That's what I thought the plan was," I say through clenched teeth. "But instead of being mature about it, you push me away. How could you, Levi? I thought we were friends."

"We are!"

I dunk my hands in the cool water again. "Seriously, I need you to get away from me right now." My voice is shaking. I'm not sure I even have the energy to swim. I'm about to cry.

When I look up and see Levi's eyes watering, I really do start crying.

Then Coach Josh is there, hugging me against his side. "What's going on?"

I'm so embarrassed and hurt I can't tell Coach the truth. A tear drips down my face. I swipe it away.

"It's my fault, Coach," Levi says.

"Get warmed up," Coach tells him, and he actually listens and leaves this time. Once he's out of my sight, I start breathing in through my nose, out through my mouth. *Strong and steady*, I tell myself.

I've been working toward this day my entire life. No boy is gonna mess that up. But then a vision of another girl touching his hip makes me cry harder. I can't help it. It doesn't matter that it was Roxy. He's right—it could've been anyone, and I'd still be freaking out.

"Tell me what happened," Coach says.

"Levi acted like a jerk." *To hurt me. To push me away.*

"Can you put it out of your mind?"

I wipe away a tear with my finger. "Trying." My voice breaks again. How could Levi do this? Do I even know him at all?

"The race is in three minutes," Coach says. "What do you want to do?"

"I'm gonna swim."

Coach squeezes my shoulder. "That a girl."

By this time, Mom is striding across the pool deck. She came down out of the stands to check on me? God. What a tidal wave of embarrassment. She pulls me into her arms and hugs me tight.

"Are you okay, Tadpole?"

"No." My voice breaks.

"Is this about Levi?"

"How'd you know?"

"I could tell things were changing between you," Mom says quietly. *Seriously, how do moms always know?*

"She's going to race," Coach says.

"Good," Mom replies with a smile, handing me some tissues. I wipe my eyes and blow my nose. I refuse to look at the other swimmers as I stretch my arms a final time.

I hop into the pool. Roxy's in the lane right next to me. As swimmers with the best prelim times, we are in the middle of the pool.

"Lovers' spat?" she asks.

I don't respond. I take a few deep breaths, grab hold of the bars above me, and prepare to push off backward. Before the buzzer sounds, I look for the Make Waves pendant that always dangles in front of me. It's not there.

The buzzer beeps. I throw myself backward, pointing my toes

so my feet don't drag, and begin my fluid stroke. Kick, kick, kick. I can see Roxy to my right. I keep my pace steady. Don't change it. Don't change it at all. Push, push, push. I flip into my first turn, nailing it. I shove off the wall as hard as I can, flip over, and dolphin kick back to the surface. My muscles are loosening up. I'm feeling more comfortable. I take a risk and increase my speed ever so slightly. I make the second and third turns fine. I'm rocking this. The other turns go smoothly too. On my last length of the pool, I have the energy. I push the tiniest bit harder. The cheering crowd is going crazy. I slap my hands against the side of the pool. The race is over.

I turn to check the scoreboard. I lost by a hundredth of a second.

I cover my mouth.

I lost. I lost to Roxy. Again. I shouldn't have lost.

If I can't win state, what business do I have being on the US Olympic team? How would I even make it past the one hundred other swimmers who already have cuts for Omaha?

Roxy turns to me and gives me a hug. I smile through pursed lips, and climb out of the pool.

"You did great," Coach Josh tells me.

"I lost."

Coach places both hands on my shoulders. "You know Katie Ledecky doesn't do as well in short course either. She loses lots of those races. You're just like her. You're going to kill it in long course next month, understand?"

I nod robotically.

"And you've still got 200 free later. I have a feeling you'll do great."

I slip my feet into my sneakers and stalk off the deck, passing Roxy celebrating with her family.

"Congratulations, Maggie!" her mom calls out. I give her a quick wave, then continue on, needing to be alone. I slide down next to a drink machine in a corner. I can't believe I lost.

To make my thoughts stop racing, I picture myself lying on a beach under the hot sun. But the image turns into one of me and Levi, playing cards on a beach towel at Normandy Lake. New, hot tears rush down my face. I can't believe what happened—I called my best friend an asshole.

While I'm hiding in the hallway, I hear Levi announced as the winner of 100 breaststroke.

That makes me smile. Even though he hurt me beyond belief, I'm still proud of him. He's the best.

So this is what heartbreak feels like.

Jenga

I hope and pray to God I'll do better in my second final of the day: 200 free.

To prepare, I stretch all my muscles and inhale deeply through my nose.

"Maggie!"

I look up from touching my toes to find Hunter and Georgia walking up. He's still in his Raiders baseball uniform, and Georgia looks comfortable in leggings and a light sweater. It's hard to believe spring is two weeks away. Normally I'd be terribly excited for warm weather and flowers blooming, but at the moment it feels like the dark of winter will never end.

"I'm so excited you guys are here," I say. "I lost."

We give each other side hugs.

"That sucks about your first race," Hunter says. "But second place is pretty amazing, Mags."

"Yeah."

Georgia touches my elbow. "Is something wrong? Levi wouldn't talk to us."

"I don't want to talk about him, okay?" I snap, startling Georgia.

Hunter pats my back, ignoring my outburst. "Can I do anything?"

"Tell me about something. Anything."

He continues rubbing friendly circles on my back. "You won't believe what happened at my baseball game today."

Georgia starts cracking up so hard her face turns red.

"I can't wait to hear this," I say.

"Shelby and I haven't had a whole lot of alone time lately because her dad won't let me come over after the pizza delivery incident, and my house is always packed." Hunter has three sisters. "I had a bit of time before the game was going to start, so Shelby and I snuck off to the equipment shed."

Georgia snorts loudly, and Hunter gives her a look.

"We were fooling around, and I guess we were a little loud and didn't notice the window was open...until the guys outside the shed started cheering us on."

"Oh my God," I say. "So now everybody on your team knows what you sound like when you're—"

"Doing the nasty?" Georgia says. "Yup."

Hunter shakes his head. "It's not nasty. It's beautiful."

"Oh my God," I say again. I'd be mortified. "Is Shelby okay?"

"No one saw us. She thought it was pretty funny, but I think she's hoping and praying it doesn't get back to her parents!"

"Maggie," Coach Josh calls. "You're up."

"Gotta go, guys. Thank you so much for coming."

They give me good luck hugs, and then I'm off. When I hit the deck, I'm not even nervous. I'm still laughing at Hunter's story. I wipe the tears from my eyes as I head over to the blocks. Levi sees me chuckling, and it makes him grin as he fingers the goggles hanging around his neck. I wipe the smile off my face.

I strip out of my sweats and down to my suit, adjust my bottoms to make sure I don't have a wedgie, and listen to Coach Josh's last minute pep talk. He squeezes my shoulders. "Listen, Maggie. You swam your personal best in this event two weeks ago. You only need to do one thing today."

"Try to improve a little?"

He smiles. "You got it."

I step up to the blocks at lane four. Roxy's in lane five. She says something, but I don't process her words. I take a few practice strokes and shake out my arms. Adjust my cap and make sure my goggles are secure. Keep my eyes focused on the water in front of me.

The buzzer beeps, and I leap.

My dive is perfect. I dolphin kick to the surface and fluidly begin my free stroke. *Elbows high, elbows high.* I count my strokes, perfectly measuring when to make my turns. On the last length of the pool, I can feel it. I have some energy left. It's a bit of improvement. I go for it. I put all my strength into my stroke, making this race mine.

On my last stroke, I slam both hands into the side of the pool to finish. I pop up out of the water to face the scoreboard.

My name is at the top!

I won! I won the state championship in 200 free!

I slap my hand on top of the water and scream along with the people cheering for me, doing a little dance in the water. This isn't usually my strongest race. I never expected this. Never!

"Nice race, Maggie," Roxy says, giving me a perfunctory hug. "See you in Huntsville next month. Tell Levi I can't wait to see him again too," she taunts, and climbs out of the pool.

Never in my life have I been so tempted to dunk someone. Instead I hop out of the water and rush for Coach Josh and my parents. Hunter and Georgia are there with big hugs. Oma, Opa, and Ms. Lucassen are all over me too.

"You were amazing!" Mom says.

"You're nearly as good as I was back in the Netherlands," Oma says.

"We'll have to celebrate with a pizza party," Opa says. *Levi's grandparents are the cutest.*

"You are crushing it in this event," Coach adds. "I think you're starting to have a better chance in free than in back."

Levi is standing a few feet away. He bites his lower lip.

Then Jason breaks the tension of the moment. "Wooo, Maggie King!" he yells, slapping my butt with a kickboard and darting off.

"Jerk!" I say.

I turn and shuffle-chase after him in my sneakers, glad for the excuse to avoid Levi.

Because he looks devastated.

Just like me.

～～

Later that night, while Mom and Dad go check on a wedding reception one of their junior associates planned, I lie on the sofa wiping tears from my eyes. I'm surrounded by a snowstorm of tissues. It reminds me of Levi's bed the other day when he was sick. Why does everything make me think of him?

I'm proud I won 200 free. Really proud. When I checked my phone, I must've had more than a hundred texts and messages from people congratulating me on winning the state championship. I did do very well.

And maybe Coach is right. Maybe I am better in 200 free than in backstroke. Not that I'm giving up back. Maybe my swimming career is just changing.

Everything's changing.

A tear slides down my cheek. No, I'm not crying about backstroke. I'm crying because the most important relationship of my life is not as strong as I thought it was. Levi hurt me to avoid having a serious conversation. If our friendship broke this easily, the rest of my life must be as fragile as a Jenga tower.

The doorbell rings. I don't bother getting up to answer it.

A minute later Levi appears in the doorway to the den.

"What are you doing here? And who said you can barge into my house like this?"

He flinches. "When you didn't answer the door, I got worried." He pointedly looks at my mess of Kleenex. He sucks in a breath. "What I did today was a total dick move. I know it."

"Yeah, it was."

He hesitates. "I'm sorry. Can you forgive me?"

"I'll always forgive you Levi, but I'm really angry with you right now. I don't know why you're here."

Levi sucks on his lower lip. "I hope I didn't mess up our friendship."

What friendship? I'm about to say, when I realize I don't want to hurt him. I pretty much hate him right now, but I want to be a bigger person than that. No one deserves to be treated like he treated me today.

I sigh. "Levi, I need a break from you for a while, okay?"

His face creases with disappointment. "Okay."

"You can let yourself out."

I bury my face in the heels of my hands, listening to the heavy fall of his footsteps. Then I'm alone, just me and the medal I won today. I'm proud of it. I really am.

But somehow it doesn't feel so special since I'm not celebrating with my best friend.

Coach gives me Sunday off.

He texted that it's a reward for winning 200 free—but he probably thinks I need some space from Levi. Which is totally true.

Church is stressful because Georgia keeps asking what happened between us. We write notes back and forth on the little offering envelopes. Her mother, who is sitting in the pew behind us, keeps clicking her tongue because writing notes in church is apparently a total sin.

Did you and Levi fight?

I will tell you, but I don't want it to affect your friendship with him.

Why would it?

I pull a deep breath and write, I had been planning to talk to him about us but he freaked out and pushed me away. He wanted to hook up with somebody else. Then Roxy flirted with him and I saw.

Georgia takes the envelope from my hand and reads the note, then folds it with crisp, angry movements.

Outside, it's a beautiful morning. One of those rare seventy-degree March days. It gets a whole lot hotter when Georgia folds her arms across her stomach.

"Levi *cheated* on you?"

"We weren't officially together, so, no, he didn't cheat."

"But you guys were fooling around, and then he tried to push you away by coming on to Roxy? That rat bastard jerk!"

"George, I told you," I say quickly. "I don't want this messing up your friendship with Levi."

"I don't want to be friends with a dick like that!"

"Georgia."

"Maggie."

"He is not like Kevin," I say gently. "Levi didn't treat me like he treated you."

"But Levi hurt you!"

"I will feel terrible if this messes up our group," I say quietly.

"Me too, but it's not our fault. It's his!"

"Actually, it's mine. I'm the one who started this whole thing."

"Don't you dare defend him! You're better than that."

"Georgia," her mother calls from the parking lot. "We need to go or we'll be late to meet your grandmother."

Georgia gives me a hug good-bye.

After church, Mom and Dad have paperwork to do at the office. By midafternoon I'm bored out of my mind—no practice, homework is done, nothing is on TV, sad thoughts won't stop racing through my mind—so I decide to walk over and see if Chef made any snacks.

When I get to Mom and Dad's office, Mom has left because of a "napkin emergency at a baby shower." What in the world is a napkin emergency?

I plop down in Dad's office, which is covered in pictures of events he designed. A picture from Shelby Goodwin's thirteenth birthday party hangs on the wall. It was held in a tent on the Goodwins' lavish horse farm. Half of the party was a black and blue nightclub for the kids, while the adult side was all gold opulence and champagne fountains. Dad pitched it as classy and cool, and the Goodwins have been hiring him to cater their parties ever since. *Take that, Diane Musgrave.*

Dad looks up from his laptop. "What are you doing here, Tadpole?"

"Came to see if you have any food."

He shuts the lid on his computer. "Chef's getting ready for an anniversary party tonight. We can probably scrounge something up."

He leads me down the hall and out back to the spacious kitchens filled with pans hanging from the ceiling, ovens, and stoves. I call out a hello to Chef, but he is in Cooking Mode and has no patience for anything except letting the bread yeast rise. Four assistant cooks rush around doing his bidding.

Dad takes a plate around the kitchen, dodging cranky cooks, stealing samples for us. He pours us each a glass of iced tea, and we sit down together on the back porch, which overlooks rolling hills to the right and cornfields to the left. What a gorgeous day. The rest of the week will be in the fifties, so it's nice to have this little reprieve. It's so sunny I put on my sunglasses.

I dig into the almonds, pita chips, and hummus Dad collected for me.

He pops an olive in his mouth. "Bad news. We lost the pajama party bid."

"Oh no," I say. "I'm so sorry, Dad. What happened?"

He shrugs, his shoulders drooping. "You know how we won the contract last year because we proposed that people wear kimonos, and we would serve sushi and Asian-American fusion?"

"Right."

"This year Diane Musgrave pitched a 'pajamas around the world party,' featuring foods from other countries," he says, making finger quotes.

"She totally one-upped your idea again! Does that woman have one original thought? Aren't you pissed?"

"Yeah, sort of." Dad snags another olive and tosses it in his mouth. "I'd proposed an Americana theme this year—hot dogs, cotton candy. Something simple but delicious." Dad loves the classics. "It turned out the mayor's office wanted something different. I can't let what other people do affect me."

"But how do you get past that?"

My father thinks for a moment. "If you spend all your time thinking about how someone is going to one-up you, you can't put your best foot forward. You can't spend all your mental energy focusing on your opponent. You'll lose every time that way."

I push the almonds around on the plate.

"Maggie, what's wrong?" Dad asks. "Your mom said something happened with Levi?"

"We had a fight."

"About what?"

I shake my head. "He did something mean. I'm not sure he was thinking straight when he did it, and he apologized. I probably overreacted—it's not all his fault, but I don't know that I can get past it."

Dad squeezes my shoulder. "Friends like Levi don't come around every day. I'm sure he didn't mean to upset you."

"It still hurts." *And it's mostly my fault.* He would've never been in that situation if not for me. "I need some time."

"Nothing wrong with a bit of distance to help you see things clearly. I was really pissed last night when I heard Musgrave won the pajama party contract, but then I thought, she won't win next year because she won't be able to copy my idea from *this* year." Dad chuckles evilly. "And I'll come up with something even better."

I love my dad.

And he's right. It's okay to take time to let the dust settle. It's okay to regroup.

On Sunday night, I make a decision.

I text Levi: I am driving myself tomorrow.

Practice

Levi looks unkempt.

At practice Monday morning, he hasn't shaved his face and his hair isn't brushed. Normally it's sleeked back before he tucks it under a swim cap.

Instead of joining me in lane six, he hops down into lane eight with Jason and two other guys. Four guys to a lane gives them less room to spread out, which causes them to roughhouse around for room. He appears to be paying for his decision to switch lanes because the guys are doing silly stuff during breaks between sets, like cannonballing into the water to splash Levi and piss him off. On top of that, they are all rapping loudly along with the music spilling from the speakers. Levi horses around on occasion, but he doesn't seem to be in the mood today—and he tells them to shut up.

Lunchtime is not any better. We join Hunter and Shelby and Shelby's gaggle of sophomore friends who are busy making fun of how they got caught going at it in the equipment shed.

"*Right there. Right there, baby!*" a girl says, mimicking Hunter's deep voice.

"*Say you're mine!*" another one cries.

"*I want to know every part of you!*"

"*I fantasize about you!*"

"*Don't stop!*"

"That is *not* what I sound like," Hunter protests.

Shelby, laughing so hard tears are rolling down her cheeks, elbows him. "It kind of is."

I cover my mouth, barely able to contain my laughter. Georgia and Levi, however, are acting weird.

Georgia is so mad at Levi she didn't even sit at our table. She's over with David and all the Quiz Bowl guys, who are busy reading questions to each other from index cards. At least Georgia will be great at playing *Jeopardy!* after this.

I spy Levi out of the corner of my eye, giving me nervous glances. He's reading a worn copy of *Divergent*. Even though lunch is half an hour long, I never see him turning a page.

"Why's Georgia not sitting with us?" Hunter asks as he plays with Shelby's hair.

"She's pissed at me," Levi pipes up.

"What'd you do?" Shelby asks.

"Something really stupid." His eyes find mine. "I regret it."

"Fix it," Hunter tells Levi, who nods. He bites on his lip. Then he shuts his paperback and leaves the cafeteria before the bell rings. This is all my fault. If I'd never propositioned him, everything would be okay. My group would be okay. *We* would be okay, and stress wouldn't be pouring out of my eyeballs.

Levi gives me space on Monday, but on Tuesday he's back swimming in our regular lane. "Morning," he grunts, seeming more like himself. "I can't share a lane with those assholes."

"Totally understand… Levi, I'm sorry if I messed things up between you and Georgia."

He shakes his head. "It's my fault, not yours. Don't worry about anything, okay?"

I tell myself that when I see Georgia I'm going to encourage her to make up with Levi. He's nothing like Kevin, who acted blameless after he cheated on her.

We go through our workout, which is a real ballbuster. Now that we're gearing up for Junior Nationals in Huntsville in three weeks, Coach has us swimming 7,500 yards to give us the endurance we'll need to swim prelims and races in several events. Between sets we're breathing heavily and barely have energy to goof off. Jason doesn't even have the strength to slap my butt with a kickboard.

Coach paces the length of the pool, calling out pointers on technique during pull drills. "Nice, Maggie. Get your elbows higher."

For a second my mind flits to Roxy. *Are my elbows as high as hers?* But then I remember what Dad said on Sunday—if I keep focusing on my rival, it'll be a self-fulfilling prophesy. The only one I should be paying attention to is myself.

The workout is hella exhausting. After my shower, I muster the energy to put on my school clothes and pull my hair back into a bushy, wet bun. At least it's warmer outside than it had been; the water droplets in my hair aren't going to freeze. I walk out of the locker room at the same time Levi does. He nods at me, jingling his keys on the way to the lot.

I climb into my dad's Honda Accord and start the ignition, taking a deep breath. I can do this. I can drive to school. I did fine yesterday. Before pulling out of the lot, I put on my seat belt. Those crash test dummies on insurance commercials wear them, so I should too. I begin the trip back to Franklin, leaning forward in my seat, driving like an old lady. If I ever become a rich, famous swimmer with loads of endorsement deals, the first thing I will invest in is a driver.

I make it off I-40 and onto the back roads, but when I hit the four-lane road in Franklin a car totally cuts me off. Shit!

I swerve to the right.

My car runs off the road.

It flies into a ditch.

My teeth crash together, rattling my head, and I lunge forward, hitting the steering wheel, my seat belt pulling me back. Ow. *Oh my God, oh my God.*

I lift my head. Spots swim in front of my eyes as I pat down my body. Wiggle my arms and feet. I'm okay. But I'm shaking, my lips trembling. The airbag didn't open, probably because I didn't hit anything. I unbuckle my seat belt.

Someone knocks on the window. It's Levi. He opens my door, crouches down, and carefully surrounds me with his arms. I lean against his chest. It's heaving up and down.

"You okay, Magpie?"

"I'm fine. Some jerk cut me off."

He sweeps a hand up and down my spine to calm me. "You're gonna be okay." His voice is calm, but his arms are trembling.

"I'm never driving again."

"You did the right thing. You got out of the way of the bad driver and didn't crash into any other cars. I'm proud of you. You're a great driver."

"How do you know?"

"I was behind you. I saw the whole thing happen. I can't believe that asshole didn't even stop to make sure you're okay." His hand cradles the side of my head as he checks my eyes. "You feel all right? Does anything hurt?"

My forehead hurt a little at first and my arms feel like they were jarred, but I'm okay. "Can you drive me home?"

"Of course."

He collects my bag out of the car and leads me to his truck, where he opens the passenger side door and helps me inside. He even calls my dad to tell him we left the car on the other side of Franklin. Dad panics, of course, and says he'll meet me at home, but he's over in the next town, and it'll take a little while for him to drive back.

Once Levi and I are on the road, he lets out a long breath and reaches over to squeeze my hand. "You scared me, Magpie."

"I'm okay."

"If anything happened to you, I wouldn't be." At the next stoplight, he rubs his eyes, then looks over at me. "You sure you're okay? Should we go to the hospital?"

I pat my body again. "I'm fine, I think, but I'll let you know."

Back at my house, he leads me to my room. He doesn't even complain about the mess as he tucks me in under the covers. He makes me take Tylenol and sip some water, and after calling the school, he lies down next to me, breathing deeply. Staring at my face, he rests a hand on my arm.

"I'm sorry, Mags. For everything."

"I know."

The air is thick with silence.

"The Rock, the pope, and Queen Elizabeth," Levi finally says. "Who's going overboard?"

Our relationship doesn't feel normal again, but this at least gives me hope we can figure out a way to be friends.

Coach Woods asks me to stay after health class one day.

I'm sure she wants to question me about my homework. Our class had to develop individual meal plans for a week, focusing on calories and grams of fat and carbs. Basically my menu consisted of protein bars, pasta, chocolate milk, and really anything I can get my hands on in Chef's kitchen. If I come into contact with a food, I generally will eat it unless it's something like frog legs. That's what I wrote on my report: *I will eat anything but frog legs.*

"Is this about my meal plan? I'm sorry I didn't follow the instructions to stay within specific fat grams but—"

"Your plan looked a lot like mine when I was your age," Coach Woods replies. "I ate all the time. Especially at Joe's All-You-Can-Eat Pasta Shack."

"Oooh. I love that place."

"I still love it, even though I shouldn't be eating like that since I don't practice every day anymore," she admits. Then she asks, "Your parents run a catering company, right?" I nod. "My fiancé and I are getting married this summer, and he's dead set on our friend Carter catering the wedding out of his taco restaurant."

"Sounds delicious."

"Right? But we can't only have tacos and tortilla chips."

"You can't?" I joke.

"Well, I need to find a groom's cake, for one. And I want to do some different appetizers. Like chicken fingers and pigs in a blanket."

"My dad loves catering 'Americana,'" I say, making finger quotes. "He's all about the classics."

"Me too," she says. "But we haven't done a very good job of planning for a tent...or silverware or plates... Really all we have planned are Carter's tacos, and Sam's sister is going to play guitar when we walk down the aisle."

I write down Dad's phone number on a piece of paper and give it to her. "You can call my dad if you want. He's really into creating themes, so if you want something special for your wedding, he can pull it off. Last summer he did a Disney-themed wedding. This summer he's doing a Harry Potter one. They're serving butterbeer."

Her eyes grow wide with excitement. "I could do a football-themed wedding?!"

"Sure, yeah, I guess," I say. "The table names could be football teams. And the signature cocktail could be an *Old Fashioned Football*."

"Ooh. How'd you come up with that?"

"I grew up with my parents," I say, and she laughs.

"By the way, congrats on winning at state," she says. "The principal was telling me we've never had anyone win a state swim meet until you and Levi."

"Thank you." I adjust my backpack on my shoulder.

I must sound a little deflated because she asks, "What's wrong?"

"Did you ever have a rival?"

Coach Woods laughs into her fist. "You won't believe it. My senior year, when I was quarterback of Hundred Oaks, this new guy, Ty, showed up wanting to join the team, and he played quarterback too."

"Oh my god."

"And he was better than me."

I gasp. "What did you do?"

"I played harder than I ever had in my life and showed him who was boss. I let him get some playing time too because I was captain and needed to give other kids opportunities, but I made sure he knew it was my team."

"That worked?"

She picks up the football from her desk and tosses it to herself. "I wanted to play. I wouldn't let anyone stand in my way."

"That guy, Ty, what happened with him? Was he upset he didn't get to play much?"

Coach Woods smirks a little. "We dated for a while. So, yeah, he was mad, but not *that* mad. And now he plays quarterback for the Arizona Cardinals. I'd say he's doing okay."

"Uh, wow."

"Why'd you ask about a rival?"

"This one girl always gets in my head. I lose to her more often than I should."

"You need to be racing yourself, not her."

"That's what Coach Josh says."

"So what's the issue?"

"I dunno…she humiliates me. She flirted with Levi—my best friend—right in front of me. She brags online that she's better than I am. She says mean things to me in person."

"Sounds like she's trying to prove she's better than you...but she's not doing it in the pool."

"She beat me at state, though."

"Were you at your best during that race?"

I shake my head. I'd been crying over a boy. I was nowhere near my best.

Coach Woods sets her football down on her desk. "Are you one of the best swimmers in Tennessee?"

I don't hesitate to say "Yes."

"You have a coach who gets up early every morning before dawn to practice with you, right?"

"Yes."

"Why?"

"He believes in me."

"And he believes in you because you're good. You wouldn't have won that race at state if you weren't an excellent swimmer. Your strength has nothing to do with your rival. It's all about you. When you're in the pool, you have to block out everything except your hard work.

"When I first met Ty, I was scared when I saw how far he could throw and that he was taller and buffer than me. But I had put in the time. My coach and team believed in me. So I believed in myself and kept playing hard and working to get better. It was all about me."

I smile at her. "I get that. I try to stay focused on improving, on my times, but sometimes I mess up and forget."

"There's only one way to fix that."

"What?"

She tosses me her football. "Practice."

Ariel and Tarzan

Coach Josh is all about keeping us lean.

He has us do a lot of high rep, low intensity weight lifting. When we were younger, we only swam and did cardio, but once we turned fourteen, Coach made us start working out with trainers twice a week at a Nashville gym.

At first, I hated it. I worried lifting would make my shoulders huge and that cute dresses wouldn't fit right anymore. But once I saw how much it toned my body and slimmed me down, I fell in love with it. On top of that, it stripped away the body issues I had in middle school. My butt looks great in a suit, and I know it.

During training, Jason is spotting me on squats. With both hands I balance a bar holding two weights across my shoulder blades. *Up I go. Down. Up I go. Down.*

I can see Levi in the mirror. He is lying on a weight bench, doing chest press with two big barbells. I try to avoid noticing how great his chest looks in that snug T-shirt.

Coach worries about swimcest because we're often in the water wearing little more than a scrap of bathing suit. But to me, the weight room—where guys act like cavemen, throwing weights around and grunting, is a lot sexier than Speedos.

"Roxy was bragging online again," Jason tells me. He still follows her on Snapchat and Twitter. "She posted a picture of you at state. Do you want to know what it said?"

Part of me does, part of me doesn't.

Levi sits up on the bench, resting two free weights on his thighs. "Maggie doesn't want to know, idiot."

"I can answer for myself." I finish my twelfth squat and place the bar back on the rack. "And no, I don't want to know."

"Are you going to tweet or compete?" Coach Josh asks from across the weight room. He hates social media almost as much as swimcest, so we have to suffer through his corny catchphrase lectures.

"Don't mention Roxy again," Levi tells Jason.

"Levi, seriously," I say.

"Less talk, more reps," Coach Josh calls.

Keeping our mouths shut is the hardest part about lifting weights. You can't talk under water. It's easy to get lost in conversation on dry land. But you should always focus in the weight room; someone could seriously get hurt if you aren't paying careful attention.

Jason adds more weight to the squat bar and moves into position. I spot him from behind. He makes it through six reps, then puts the bar down with a loud grunting sigh.

"You okay?" I ask. He was supposed to do twelve reps. "Dehydrated?"

"My heart's not in it today."

"What's wrong?" I ask quietly.

"Dad got pissed I came in second at state to Levi and didn't place in my other events. He said I'm a fuckup."

"But you beat Levi at regionals. Your dad was happy about that. I saw him slapping your back and celebrating."

"He *was* happy, and now he's not."

"I'm sorry."

Jason does the same workouts we do every single day but has never seemed as focused as Levi and me. Sometimes I wonder if his heart is in it at all. It has to be, to compete at this level. But I've often thought it was his father who was invested, not Jason. I mean, I'd never tweet something like, "God I hate swim practice!" which Jason has been known to do.

Nobody's forcing me to swim. I love it. I want to keep doing it in college and maybe even professionally—if I'm good enough.

"Jason," Coach Josh calls. "Quit dogging it. Get back to work."

With blank eyes, Jason finishes the other six reps.

After removing the extra weights he used, I step back up to the squat bar. Through the mirror, I can see Levi still sitting on a weight bench staring my way.

He watches me as I go up and down.

I tell myself he's probably watching my form, making sure I don't hurt myself.

Secretly I wish he was staring at me for more romantic reasons. It's been two weeks since we last kissed. I miss it. I miss him. But I care more about Junior Nationals in Huntsville next weekend than romance.

I'd been willing to figure out how to balance swimming and a relationship, but Levi wasn't brave enough to even have that conversation. I'm not putting myself out there again for someone who wasn't willing to simply talk.

I finish my reps and set the squat bar back on the rack. Breathing deeply, I catch my breath and wipe the sweat off my forehead with a towel.

Our eyes meet in the mirror.

I can't let him distract me, no matter how much I wish he would.

It's five days until Junior Nationals.

My first opportunity this year to get an Olympic trial cut and Levi's first opportunity to prep for the trials in a long course meet. We both have a lot at stake.

Monday afternoon after practice, Coach calls me into his office to watch a video. He makes me sit in the chair behind his computer as he works the mouse beside me. Footage of a meet appears on the screen, but I don't recognize any of the swimmers.

"Who's this?" I ask.

"This girl won the Indiana 200 back state championship. You'll be up against her at Junior Nationals."

I watch the video. She's on fire, tooling across the surface of the water, but her finish time was an entire second slower than mine!

The next day, Coach calls me in to watch another YouTube video. It's another swimmer, the girl who won the Washington state 200 freestyle race. My time was half a second faster.

Coach keeps up this routine all week, including during our van ride to Huntsville. Seven of us qualified to compete in this meet, so it's a rowdy trip with the guys telling raunchy jokes and threatening to moon other cars and Susannah and me yelling at them to stop. From behind the wheel, Coach tells me to look up a particular swimmer on YouTube who lives in California and did very well at her state championships. I watch a couple of her recent videos. My times are comparable to hers.

"Okay, I get it. I'm good."

Coach Josh smiles at me in the rearview mirror. "I'm glad you believe it."

When we get to Huntsville, Coach checks us into our hotel rooms and tells us to meet in the lobby in fifteen minutes for dinner and a team meeting. As far as hotels go, this one's pretty nice. My bed looks comfy and clean. I should sleep well here.

After Susannah and I finish getting settled in our room, we take the elevator back downstairs. With so many teams here, there's a lot going on and plenty of people to check out. Guys from other teams say hi to Susannah and me as we walk by. I smile, feeling more confident than I used to around boys. I'm not interested in hooking up with anybody—this meet is way too important to me, but my lessons with Levi paid off in terms of my confidence. Physically, I know what I'm doing with boys now.

Out of the corner of my eye, I keep a look out for Roxy. Then I shake my head and think about the videos Coach showed me and my new gold state championship medal for 200 free that's hanging from the vanity in my bedroom. I'm not going to concentrate on her anymore.

I'm going to focus on the qualifying cuts for the trials: 2:02:39 for 200-meter free and 2:16:59 in 200-meter back.

On top of that, Coach Josh is putting me in the prelims for 50/100/200 in free and back, just to see how I do. I am pumped.

Coach drives us to a nearby pizza place for dinner, where the waiter is thrilled to serve a bunch of boys and girls who eat entire pizzas on their own.

While waiting for our food to arrive, Jason decides to conduct a Twitter poll on his phone. He posts: Which Speedo should I wear tomorrow?

- Red
- Black

- Purple
- Pink

We all get out our phones and start voting for pink. By the time our pizza comes, he has three hundred votes, and pink is winning at 90 percent.

Once we are carbed up for tomorrow, it's team meeting time. *Otherwise known as a lecture on common sense.*

Coach looks at each of us one by one. "You've worked hard to get here. Don't screw it up. Everyone better be in bed by nine o'clock tonight. I'll be checking your rooms. And no sneaking out." Coach looks pointedly at Jason, who's rooming with Levi.

Back at the hotel after Coach does his room checks, Susannah climbs out of bed. She strips off her pajamas and wiggles into a black mini dress.

"Are you really going out?" I ask.

She slips on a pair of strappy black sandals. "Did you see that guy from Dallas? Jon? He is so hot. He said his team is sneaking out to a club."

"Wouldn't you rather wait until the meet is over?"

"That's four days from now! He might meet someone else." She spritzes perfume on her neck and checks her lip gloss one last time. "Wish me luck!"

"You're out of your mind!" I call as the door clicks shut.

Shaking my head, I turn off the lights, fall backward onto my pillow that I brought from home, and stare at the ceiling. Sleep. I want to sleep. But I'm totally amped up. I didn't work out today and have way too much leftover energy. Maybe I should jump on the bed or something. Coach would probably say that's an unsanctioned activity.

My phone buzzes. It's a text from Levi: What are you doing?

Me: Lying here trying to fall asleep. Susannah snuck out.

Levi: Oh yeah? Jason invited some girl over and now they're in bed.

Me: With you in the room?

Levi: He is an exhibitionist.

Me: Ick.

Levi: You're telling me. It's like Cirque du Soleil over here.

I cringe.

Levi: Can I come over?

His words shock me so much I accidentally drop my phone on my face. It hits me in the chin. Ow. I scramble to pick it back up. Does he want to come over to get away from Jason? Or does he want to spend alone time with me? The romantic part of me wants that; the realistic side says nope.

Dad always says "Don't plan to serve a Baked Alaska when an ice cream sundae will do." In other words, sometimes the simple solution is best. Levi probably only wants to get away from Jason's sexual circus.

I text him back. Okay.

A minute later, Levi appears at my door, barefoot, wearing

a comfortable gray T-shirt, track pants, and a ball cap flipped backward. He's carrying his own blue pillow from home. I let him in. I'm in a stretchy tank top and pajama shorts. I notice that Levi goes out of his way not to look directly at me.

We've hung out alone in our hotel rooms on trips before, but not since we started hooking up. How do I make this less awkward? Offer him a snack from the minibar? Isn't that how people come on to each other in movies? I can't do that. Plus, when Susannah was rooting through the minibar earlier, she found plenty of options for contraception. I decide not to explore the minibar.

"Want to watch something on TV?" I ask with a thick voice, and he nods. I flick on the TV and scroll through the guide. I stop on *Tangled*, my favorite Disney movie.

We lie down on the bed next to each other, like we used to at his house. After tossing his cap on the foot of the bed, he stretches an arm behind his head, propping himself up so he can see the screen. I lie on my side. Two feet of space stretches out between us, but it's not far enough. I can still hear his steady breathing. If I listened hard enough, could I hear his heart?

He yawns. I yawn. It's eleven o'clock. This is way later than we normally stay up at home. It sucks that Jason and Susannah are messing up our schedule.

"I can't sleep," I say. "I need to get some rest or I'm gonna be a wreck in the morning."

"Me too… C'mere," he says, reaching out to me.

I stare at his extended arm. "What are you doing?"

"Let me try to help you get to sleep."

We've done this before. When my cat died a couple years ago, Levi came over to comfort me while I cried, and he held me until I finally dozed off. We've napped together too. But this feels different. He's not simply a human pillow. He's a human pillow with whom I recently got very physical.

I curl up in the crook of his arm, resting my cheek on his warm chest, shutting my eyes.

"If you could be any Disney princess, which one would you be?" he asks softly.

"Ariel, obviously. I'd be a great mermaid. Which prince would you be?"

"Tarzan, duh."

"Tarzan isn't a prince."

"But he's a Disney hero. And he wears a loin cloth, just like me."

I snort, and snuggle closer to him. A few weeks ago, I would've been taking off his clothes and kissing his neck. This would have been our first time alone in a hotel room since I propositioned him. I probably would've been thinking about bananas and condoms from the minibar and whether I was ready for that.

But now—I think back to the ice cream sundae and forget the Baked Alaska. I clear my head, warm and relaxed in his arms, and drift to sleep.

I wake up to the door slamming shut. My eyes blink open to

find Susannah standing there in her black dress with mussed hair and smeared mascara.

"Holy shit," she says, gaping at us, wobbly in her heels.

Levi and I are completely wrapped around each other like two starfish. We sit up, sheets falling down around our waists.

I rub my eyes. "What time is it?"

"Two thirty." Susannah reaches for the doorknob. "Did I interrupt you guys? I can come back."

"We were sleeping," I say.

"I'll go back to my room," Levi says, yawning as he rolls out of bed cradling his pillow in his arms. "Maybe the circus is over now."

After waving bye to him, I curl up under the covers and shut my eyes. With the TV off, the room is silent—until Susannah goes and breaks it.

"Seriously. Did you guys do it?"

I sigh, desperate for some rest. "No."

"Have you done it?"

"No," I say a little more forcefully.

She squeals a little and kicks her feet up and down. "But you're totally going to! I always knew you guys would get together."

First Georgia, now Susannah. I don't even bother telling her been there, done that, and it's over.

Because it is over.

But God, did it feel good in his arms.

It takes a long time for me to fall back asleep.

Morning comes way too early. Not as early as I normally get up for the drive to Nashville but still early. We don't have a practice—it's straight to the races.

As I'm putting on my blue and white New Wave sweats, Levi texts me, asking to meet up. I finish getting ready, grab my bag, and take the elevator downstairs, trying to ignore the knots in my stomach. This is a big week.

In the lobby I find him sitting on a sofa, bent over tying his tennis shoes, a piece of toast hanging out of his mouth.

"Morning," I tell him quietly.

He takes a bite of the toast and smiles at me. "Sleep good?"

"Not my best." I sit down next to him and check my phone. "You?"

"I slept better in your room. Once Jason got rid of the circus performer, he fell asleep and started snoring as usual."

"Hey, Maggie! Hey, Levi!" a voice calls. I look up, and Roxy is walking across the lobby with the Memphis Marines in their green sweats. She gives me a smile and a wave.

I ignore her. So does Levi. He glances over at me and swallows.

Whatever. I can't let her—or him—affect me today.

Coach Josh drives us to the Huntsville Springs Natatorium, where the four-day meet is taking place. This meet is longer than the high school meets back in Tennessee because a lot more people will be competing in the preliminary heats. First up today are prelims for breaststroke, which I'm not swimming, so I have some downtime. I stand at the end of Levi's lane and cheer for him during the 100 preliminary, where he breaks his seed time and gets put into a faster heat for the semifinal. That is amazing considering the level of swimmers at this meet.

These are the best young swimmers in the United States.

Later in the day, he comes in fifth place at the final. Club swimming is a whole lot tougher than going against kids back in Tennessee. Plus, he complains that his ankle is tight. Levi's disappointed; he swam the race of his life but didn't get cuts to qualify for 100 breast at the trials. He is hoping to qualify for more than one event at the trials in Omaha. At least he'll have two more tries in Atlanta and Cincinnati.

Coach has me do prelims for butterfly that afternoon, but I'm not competitive in the stroke. I don't even qualify to move on to the A final. I'm placed in the D group.

That evening, I have way too much energy. During free time, Jason and Susannah convince me to walk down the street to play minigolf. Minigolf is a sanctioned activity because, according to Coach, very little can go wrong in minigolf. I mean, unless somebody rockets a ball at your forehead.

Levi is too tired to go along and wants to ice his ankle. Truth be told, after last night I'm relieved to be apart from him. At least for a little while.

Of course, as I'm aiming my golf ball down the green past a

little windmill, Susannah brings up last night. "So what were you and Levi doing in bed together?"

I lose control of my club, and the ball goes way off course, missing the hole and bouncing off the brick ledge.

"Just sleeping," I say.

"You and Levi are sleeping together?" Jason blurts.

"No! I mean, yes, we were sleeping together, but not *sleep* sleeping together. *Resting*." Aggravated, I shake my head. "Look, we're not doing it." ·

Jason makes perverted movements with his golf club. "Bow-chicka-wow-wow."

I roll my eyes.

After one game, I regret coming out with them because they suddenly appear to be the horniest people ever. They will not stop making comments about mine and Levi's nonexistent sex life. So I decide to head back to the hotel on my own while they stay for another round of golf.

The hotel lobby is filled with swimmers gossiping and having a good time. I pass a group of guys who say hi, returning their smiles, but continue on to the elevator and ride up to my floor. I need some sleep. My prelims for 100/200 backstroke start tomorrow morning at nine.

As I get off the elevator, I see movement down the corridor from my room. Levi is standing outside his door with an ice bucket under his arm, chatting with a pretty girl who has long black hair and swims for the Atlanta Bullets. I think her name is Kara. He's smiling at whatever she's saying. He didn't play minigolf because he wanted some rest...but he has the energy to flirt?

She leans closer to him, and he doesn't stop her. I can't watch this. I shove my key card in the reader, push my door open, and shut it quietly before he sees me.

Shaking with disbelief, I let out a sob into my hands. I never expected to become jealous like this—a girl who cries over a boy. Then again, I didn't expect to grow feelings for him. My chest hurts so much my heart must be breaking in two.

After putting on pajamas and climbing into bed, I work to keep my tears at bay by biting on my lower lip. I can't cry. It's too dangerous. My tears might drain into my throat and chest, causing me to get sick before my races tomorrow.

Maybe he's not hooking up with her. Maybe he went into his room and she went back to hers, and now he's reading that urban fantasy novel about werewolves using a dating service in New York that he was so excited about, and she's calling her boyfriend back home because she was never interested in Levi in the first place.

I need to know.

So I send him our usual bedtime text: Good night

My phone rests on the bed next to me. I keep waiting for it to light up. But the text doesn't come for over an hour.

Good night, M

He could have been doing anything in that time, I tell myself, but most likely he was kissing a girl who is not me.

I can't fall asleep for hours. It's not his fault I developed deeper feelings for him. He is allowed to live his life, and that means kissing whoever he wants. Still, it sucks big time. It also sucks that I've been obsessing over a guy when I should be focused on my sport. What was I thinking?

The next morning in the lobby, I read my parents' encouraging good luck texts while I pick at my protein bar. It tastes like dirt. Levi joins me right as I'm finishing the food I'm not hungry for. He has bags under his eyes. Was he up all night with that girl?

With ginger movements, Levi lowers his bag to the floor, sits down next to me, and starts rotating his foot in slow circles.

"How does it feel?" I ask.

"Stiff. A little sore, but not bad."

"Are you going to swim today?"

"I dunno. Doesn't seem worth it to swim free and butterfly since I already swam breast yesterday."

I get that. Rather than risk further straining his ankle, it may be better to start fresh in Atlanta in a few weeks.

He lets out a long sigh, rubbing his eyes.

"You okay?" I ask.

"I'm sick of Jason. He had that girl over again last night."

"Didn't you have somebody over too?"

He gives me a look of surprise. "No. I didn't. Why'd you think that?"

"I saw you in the hall with that girl from the Atlanta Bullets."

From his bag, he passes over a carton of chocolate milk he picked up for me. "Oh. Yeah. We were just talking."

"Oh. It took you forever to answer my text last night."

"I was exhausted because of my foot and passed out early without meaning to. I answered your text when Jason woke me up."

My face flushes. "I'm sorry I jumped to conclusions."

"I haven't been with anybody, Maggie."

I'm so relieved, I let out a big sigh, and he totally notices.

Levi's eyebrows pinch together as he studies my face. "You were scared I was with her?"

I nod, muttering, "This is weird."

He hasn't slept with another girl. Yet. But it will happen. He won't stay celibate forever. Leaning my head back against the couch, I stare at the ceiling.

Levi scooches closer and pats my hand. "We'll figure it out. You're my best friend, okay?"

Susannah comes and flops down in a chair across from us. "You two doing it yet?"

Levi starts coughing into his fist.

"I told you," I reply. "We're not doing it."

Coach Josh appears behind us. "Nobody is doing anybody— it's time to go. Get in the van."

As we're carrying our bags outside, Susannah elbows me. "If I were you, I'd be hitting that."

"Seriously, stop," I say, and she nods, hopefully understanding that she's hurting me.

At the pool, I take a shower and start stretching. I have my prelims for back this morning at nine, and if I qualify for any finals, they start tonight at five. This is what I've been working toward my whole life. All that matters is how I swim today.

Levi and I cheer for Jason and Susannah during their prelims, and then it's my turn to warm up. I splash into the practice lane. Coach Josh walks along the side, watching my form. I'm feeling good, especially since this is long course, and I have room to stretch out and increase my speed in the middle of the race when other swimmers start to fade. This is my favorite.

For 200 back prelims, I'm put into a very fast group thanks to my seed time. I hop into the water and reach up to grab the bars so I can launch myself into the race.

I'm in lane seven. Three lanes down in lane four is Katarina Ericson, who is only nineteen but already had a spot on the Olympic team four years ago. I can't believe I'm swimming against her. This race is simply a warm up for her, as she prepares for the Olympics in August. I'm sure she'll get a spot on the team again. It's humbling that I'm simply working to get a *tryout for a tryout* for the US Olympic team.

Don't drag your feet, don't drag your feet, I chant to myself.

The buzzer sounds, I launch backward—toes pointed, and swim my heart out. Out of the corner of my eye I spot Katarina pulling ahead. Nothing's worse than seeing people go by you when you can't make your legs go any faster.

After four lengths of the pool, I finish the race and swirl around to check my times on the scoreboard. I come in third behind Katarina and Roxy. My time is 2:17.30. Seven-tenths of a second behind what I need to qualify for the trials. I groan under my breath. It's not terrible, but not good enough either. I need to shave off almost an entire second if I want to be competitive. And the swimmers at this level are insanely competitive. At these elite long course meets, you'll often see three or four swimmers get their cuts in a single race.

Later that day at the A final, it's basically a repeat of that morning's heat. I manage to get a 2:17:25, which is slightly better, but I come in third place again. In addition to winning the race, Katarina's time qualifies her for Omaha, even though she already probably qualified in an earlier race. I lean my head against the wall, panting hard, pissed at myself. Sometimes I feel like I'm the only person not getting my cuts. That's not true, but still.

"Wooo, Maggie!"

I look up to find Coach, Levi, and the rest of my team cheering me on. I beam up at them.

I climb out of the pool, and Levi sweeps me into his arms. "Third place!"

"You're getting better and better," Coach says. "We'll shave that time off."

Eventually, I think. But will it be in time to qualify?

Outside the locker room after a shower, I meet up with Levi so we can grab the van back to the hotel. That's when someone touches my shoulder. Katarina Ericson. "You're good. Great race."

I beam at her, and Levi goes all wide-eyed as she walks off.

"Wow, none of the big guys have ever said something like that to me," he says. "We should celebrate."

"With a pizza party?" I tease, mimicking his grandparents.

Levi smiles easily. "If that's what you want."

"What I really need is a nap and a smoothie."

"You got it, boss." Levi picks up my bag to carry it for me.

It's not until I'm back at the hotel, changing into jeans and a long-sleeved tee, that I realize I haven't thought about Roxy once.

I smile at myself in the mirror and dry my hair.

Making Waves

I didn't qualify in Huntsville.

The next day at the meet, I swam 200 free and did even better than I had in back the day before. I missed the qualifying time by two-tenths of a second, which is a lot more manageable than seven-tenths. I came in third place overall. The good news? I beat Roxy! She came in eighth in 200 free. I didn't do so well in 50 or 100—but that's okay. Coach says the shorter races aren't my forte.

Deep down, though, I worry I will never qualify.

With two more chances, the Atlanta Classic in April and the Spring Spotlight in May, swimming is all I can think about. To be honest, I'm barely thinking about graduation, which is less than two months away. It's just swim, swim, swim, swim, swim.

Okay, okay, I admit I *have* been thinking a little bit about prom.

When I think back to the ridiculous bucket list Hunter made for me, part of me wishes I had more hours in the day to obsess about a dance or get excited about graduation and college. I'm lucky I have a few good friends and great parents. Without them, my life would basically be water and that's it. Hell, I spent my entire spring break in Huntsville at Junior Nationals with no beach in sight.

At least I have off the night of the pajama party at the end of the month. I decide I could pretend *that's* prom. I'm sure in some alternate universe people wear pajamas to elegant events.

One Friday night when I'm driving myself to Jiffy Burger, I realize it's April 1. And yes, that means it's only two weeks until the Atlantic Classic, but it's an important date for another reason.

At the diner, I slide into the booth next to Hunter. Georgia sandwiches him in on his other side.

"It's only two months until you leave!" I say, hugging him. "Waahhh."

He puts an arm around my shoulder and the other around Georgia. "I promise to call you."

"Do they even let you have cell phones at boot camp?" Georgia asks.

"They do, but you can only make calls if you're being supervised."

Levi arrives in time to say, "Guess that means no phone sex."

"Shut up, man."

Levi sits down on the other side of the booth away from the three of us. "I feel so left out," he jokes. "Why am I sitting alone?"

Hunter chimes in, "We've staged an intervention. You need to stop whacking off all the time."

"Ugh!" Georgia and I say.

Our usual waitress comes to take our order. I get up and

move to my spot by Levi. I elbow his arm and smile at him sideways. One side of his mouth quirks up as we dive into our usual conversation.

Georgia and David are seeing each other now, so our Jiffy Burger chats aren't only about Hunter and Shelby's sexcapades.

Tonight I even have news of my own.

"Noah Thompson asked me to go to the pajama party with him," I announce. Levi had been in the process of taking a bite of his cheeseburger when I say this. He pauses, then sets his burger on his plate.

"Eeep!" Georgia says. "What happened?"

I tell my friends how it went down earlier that day. Levi, who's playing with his fries, never lifts his head during my story. Which is a pretty boring story as far as stories go. Noah walked up to me in the hallway. He smiled. He said, "Do you want to go to the pajama party with me?"

I had to think about it for a moment because he's not the first person I would've chosen. But maybe I needed to consider other guys.

"Yeah," I told Noah. "I'll go."

He grinned. "Awesome, I'll pick you up at eight."

I attend the party every year, but I've never taken a date. Some girls wear lacy negligees or short shorts, but I always wear long plaid pants and a T-shirt. I need something cuter to wear for Noah.

He's a nice, cute guy but I don't have much interest in kissing him or anything. I don't know if that's because I don't want to kiss *him*, or I miss kissing Levi.

God, what's wrong with me? Why can't my heart listen to my mind? Levi and I are over. We were never together to begin with. He doesn't want a girlfriend. If he did, he would've been willing to talk about us.

Today after I agreed to go to the pajama party, Noah took my hand in the hallway, and it felt like I was finally getting some of the high school experience. The real stuff, not the crazy shit on Hunter's bucket list.

Levi doesn't say much during dinner. I wish I knew what he was thinking. Is he upset because he hates Noah or sad because he misses me?

On the Saturday before the Atlanta Classic, which starts on Tuesday, Levi has an appointment for a massage.

He wanted to try acupuncture to treat his stiff ankle, but Coach Josh said no way, he's not trying something new this close to a meet.

Georgia went to Knoxville for a full-day practice camp with the University of Tennessee cheerleading squad.

On top of that, there's no Saturday afternoon swim practice because the team is tapering, so I decide to go watch Hunter's baseball game against Fayetteville.

At the Hundred Oaks ballpark behind the school, I choose a seat in the stands. It's a gorgeous sunny day, though gusty winds are making knots of my hair.

It feels a little awkward sitting here by myself. It's starting to get real that my friends and I are going to be apart. Instead of Levi picking me up every morning, I'll be walking to the pool. No more Friday night trips to Jiffy Burger with Georgia and Hunter and Levi except for when we're on break from college. But I'm excited to work with one of the best college swimming coaches in the country. It's exciting and sad all at once.

Right before the game is about to start, Shelby Goodwin appears at the bottom of the stands, peering up at the rows as if trying to decide where to sit. She sees me and heads my way. I don't know how she does it, but she always manages to look cute, no matter the weather. Her blond hair is flat-ironed and doesn't appear the least bit affected by the wind, and she's wearing ripped jeans, dirty boots, a plaid shirt, and sunglasses. Her family owns a horse farm, so I imagine she spent the morning working out the horses.

"Can I sit with you?" she asks, and I nod.

Hundred Oaks is taking the field as she settles down beside me. The players run out to their positions as Hunter makes his way to the pitcher's mound at his own pace. The game can't start without him. He pounds his fist into his glove, breaking it in. Hunter gazes over at the stands, catching sight of us, and waves with a big smile on his face.

"He's glad you're here," I tell her.

She nods somberly and looks away from me, picking at her thumbnail. "I know what you guys must think of me."

"I worry my friend is going to get hurt, but he can make his own decisions. And you can do whatever you want with a guy you like."

"I do like him… I might even *more* than like him, you know? But I'm a sophomore. I have two years left of high school, and he's leaving for Colorado… You don't know how bad I wish we were the same age."

"I get that."

"It just doesn't seem realistic that we'd be happy so far apart from each other. And I want the next two years of high school to be awesome. My brother and his girlfriend can barely stand being apart long enough to go to class. I can't imagine being happy when the guy I love is so far away…" Her voice chokes up a little.

To me, it seems like, for Shelby, having a good time in high school is more important than trying to have a long-distance relationship. And that's okay. We only experience high school once. It's up to her to decide how to spend it.

I always feel bad for Jason because he's swimming his life away when he'd rather be doing something else. I can't fault Shelby for taking care of herself—her wants and needs.

When I look back on this time of my life, I know I'll be glad that swimming was the cornerstone, but also that I had great friends. I chose this life for myself. Shelby should be allowed to choose her life too, like Hunter's made his own decision to go to the Air Force Academy. If he wants to continue spending time with Shelby on her terms, I can't stop him.

"What's happening with you and Levi?" Shelby asks as a player from Fayetteville steps up to the plate, tapping his bat against his cleats.

"We're getting back to normal."

Hunter pulls off his ball cap, wipes the sweat from his brow, and secures it back in place. He cleans the baseball off on his pants and stares the batter down.

"Are you okay with that?" Shelby asks.

She's been honest with me, so I decide to do the same. "I'm not sure."

"Do you not want to do the long-distance thing either? I mean, you're going to California, and he'll be in Texas. That's huge."

I shrug a little. "I've thought about how much I'll miss him, but I haven't really thought about making a long-distance relationship work, to be honest. It's not like we're together."

Levi was right—things were intense between us. Yes, I'm going to the pajama party with Noah Thompson, but it's not like I picture myself kissing him. When I was getting lessons from Levi, there was no other guy I was practicing for. It was only him.

But if you're truly interested in somebody, you wouldn't let coaches or parents or the fact you're on the same team stop you from dating, right? I was ready to have that talk. He wasn't. I need to accept that and move on already.

"I think if Levi and I were together," I say slowly, "I'd deal with the fact we're in different states."

"Somebody's in love," she sings with a smile.

"We're not in love. If he'd truly wanted me, he would've talked to me—instead of pushing me away. He would've been mature about it."

"Maybe. Maybe not," Shelby says, cleaning her sunglasses on her shirt tail. "Guys do dumb stuff sometimes."

"Oh yeah?"

"Yeah. Did Hunter tell you how he pretended to deliver a pizza just to visit me? I was joking when I suggested it. I never imagined he'd actually do it!"

Shelby and I crack up.

Out on the field, the count is 3–2. Hunter winds up and hurls the ball right down the middle of home plate.

"Strike three!" the ump calls, and the stands erupt with cheers.

Hunter grins as he runs off the field and waves up at us again. I peek at Shelby out of the corner of my eye. Her smile is trembling.

Sacrifice sucks, but sometimes it's necessary to get what you truly need.

The Atlanta Classic swim meet will take place over three days, and one of them is my birthday.

I'm turning eighteen.

Coach Josh checks us into our hotel and gives us the usual lecture about not doing anything stupid. No sneaking out after nine. No parties in our rooms. No ordering so much Chinese takeout you can barely move the next day. (He looked directly at Jason with that one.)

So when somebody starts banging on my door after midnight, I am incredibly pissed. Susannah didn't go out for once and was fast asleep hours ago, so she's mad too.

"Go away!" she hollers, burrowing under her covers.

I pad to the door in bare feet and look out the peephole to find Levi and Jason.

I open the door.

"Happy birthday!" they yell.

Jason passes me one of those big balloons you buy at the grocery store. It's the pink Power Ranger.

"Thanks, Jason."

He playfully punches me on the shoulder and goes to jump on Susannah's bed, flopping all over her to be annoying, making her screech. I cringe. Her screams may wake up the whole hotel.

Levi sets the gift bag he's carrying on the floor, embraces me in a long hug, and gently kisses my cheek in a friendly way. "Happy birthday."

Being in his arms feels so nice I let go of the balloon, and it floats to the ceiling.

"This is going to make me sound like a dick," he starts, "But hear me out. I got myself something for your birthday."

He reaches inside his T-shirt and fishes out his chain with the Make Waves pendant. He's added a second one—a small silver disc. Looking more closely I see that it says Maggie, alongside an etching of a bear. That's the Cal mascot. I grin really big.

"Thanks," I say quietly, touching the pendant with a fingertip. "That means a lot to me."

"I got you this too." He gives me the gift bag, which I open to find the soft gray sweatshirt with his name on it in cursive. *Lucassen.* I bring it to my nose, loving its smell of cedar and his aftershave.

I cuddle his favorite shirt in my arms. "You're sure?"

"I want you to have it when you're at college."

Jason chooses that moment to start a pillow fight with Susannah. She picks up her own to clock him on the head. "Get out of here, asshole!"

"Sorry," Levi says to me. "I didn't want to bring him, but he really wanted to give you that balloon."

A loud knock pounds on the door. I open it to find Coach Josh standing there looking equal parts pissed and tired. He even has his visor on.

"Coach, do you wear your visor to bed?" Jason asks.

He sets his hands on his hips. "What are you all doing?"

"It's my fault," Levi replies. "I wanted to bring Maggie her birthday gift."

"Did you forget I was staying right next door?" Coach asks.

Jason takes the opportunity to bop Susannah on the head again with a pillow.

"Jason. Keller," Coach says. "Get your butt back to your room."

Jason tosses the pillow back on the bed. "Cooaaach," he whines like a fourth grader. Coach points at the door. Jason mopes out without another word.

Susannah smiles smugly and crawls back under the blankets and shuts her eyes.

"C'mon, Lucassen," Coach says.

"Happy birthday," Levi tells me, and pats my arm.

When he's gone, I slip his sweatshirt on over my tank top. It's so cozy soft and warm and smells like him. Almost as if I'm in his arms.

Going to sleep after that is easy.

The next day, Levi is on fire.

If he hadn't already committed to Texas, every college scout in the country would be all over him at the Atlanta Classic.

It all starts with 100 breaststroke. He wins his prelim a full length ahead of his competitors! Then, in the final, Levi leads the lanes.

Coach Josh grabs my elbow as we watch the race, both of us staring at the clock. 1:03.69 is the time he needs to make his cuts. He is totally going to beat that time. When he sails in at 1:02.90, I am jumping up and down, screaming my butt off. Coach Josh is squatting down, covering his face. Ten years of working with Levi just paid off in the biggest way.

Now Levi gets to compete in two races at trials! Both 100 and 200 breast. Two chances to make the Olympic team!

When Levi turns and sees the scoreboard, he rips off his cap and goggles and climbs out of the pool. He's shaking as he folds his arms around me in a long hug. I'm so proud of him.

Once we're off the pool deck and out in the foyer, he digs in his bag for his phone.

He wraps an arm around my waist, and I listen in as he calls his mom, Oma, and Opa to tell them. Their screams pour out of the phone.

I don't get my cuts during the meet, but it's okay because my best friend got his.

Sink or Swim

Levi drops me off at King's Royal Engagements after weight lifting one afternoon.

I wave hi to the receptionist and head back toward Mom's office, but I don't make it there because I hear laughing and arguing coming from the dining room where my parents do tastings for prospective clients.

I poke my head in to see what's happening and find Coach Woods sitting there with Dad and five other people.

"Hi," I say. "What's going on?"

"Jordan and Sam dropped by for a tasting," Dad says, beaming. When I told him Coach Woods was interested in having him plan her wedding, he went nuts. Not only does he love having the business, her dad was a famous quarterback for the Tennessee Titans, Dad's favorite football team. I'm not sure how much Mr. Woods cares about design elements and feng shui, but Dad sure is happy to tell him all about it.

Dad introduces Coach Woods' parents, her fiancé, Sam, and

his mom and dad. Their parents start asking me tons of questions about swimming—they seem really into sports. Meanwhile, Coach Woods and Sam are hovering over a platter of Chef's chocolate truffles, popping them in their mouths like M&M's and groaning about how good they are.

Mr. Woods throws his head back and stares at the ceiling. "Do either of you ever stop eating?"

"Dad, these truffles are so good!" Coach Woods exclaims.

"Jordan, we have to get a truffle display," her fiancé says.

"Can we try some?" Mrs. Woods asks, but by that point, her daughter and future son-in-law have eaten them all.

Coach Woods turns to Dad, still chewing her final chocolate. "Can the truffles be shaped like footballs?"

"Of course." Dad makes a note on his iPad, and the parents start shaking their heads, exasperated.

"How about we talk color themes?" Mrs. Woods asks. "And let's look beyond the Titans colors."

"But I had my heart set on the groomsmen wearing football uniforms," Coach Woods jokes.

"And the bridesmaids will be in cheerleading skirts," Sam replies.

Coach Woods punches his shoulder, which makes him laugh and kiss her.

"Let's compromise," Sam says to his fiancé. "You can wear the cheerleading outfit on our honeymoon."

The parents roll their eyes.

I leave them to their planning and go back to Mom's office. She's busy playing with one of her Pinterest boards online. She posts a picture of the baby shower she catered a couple weeks ago, specifically the yellow place mats and the individual tiny white flower arrangements at each place setting.

I sit down across from her.

"Hey, Tadpole." The sweatshirt I'm wearing with Levi's name on it catches her attention. "Is that Levi's?"

I feel myself blushing. "He gave it to me for my birthday."

"You guys made up?"

"Not specifically," I say. "But we're back to normal."

Mom clicks the mouse on her laptop. "That's how it is with good friends. Actually, that's how it is between your dad and me."

"Really?"

"You know we argue all the time," Mom says with a fond smile.

"Yeah, but it's about little stuff. Like what to name your aioli sauce."

"I think we get along so well because we fight about the things that bother us, rather than stewing about them."

"Levi and I had a big fight," I say. "We'd never really had a little one."

Mom turns away from her laptop to concentrate on me. "The good news is that you've made it through a bad fight. Your friendship is solid, and if you have another one—though I hope you don't—you both will be okay."

"I hope so too."

"But why are you wearing his sweatshirt? That seems like an awfully couple-y gift."

I blush. "I've wanted this for years. He probably got sick of me trying to steal it."

She raises an eyebrow. "Like I said, it seems very couple-y. It reminds me of how your dad gave me his college ring."

"It's just a sweatshirt."

She smiles knowingly. "Whatever you say, Tadpole."

After mooching dinner from the sample Americana food Dad is proposing for the Woods-Henry wedding, I walk down the street to my house. It's finally that time of year when the sun doesn't go down before I get home. As I walk, I stare at the pink and purple cotton candy sunset, and bring Levi's sweatshirt to my nose. It still smells like him. At some point I will have to wash it, but I'm not ready to yet.

Later that night, Levi texts me when I'm already in bed. It's only eight o'clock, but I'm exhausted from lifting weights today. Coach Josh is so evil I often discover muscles I didn't know I had. Like, why is my left inner thigh on fire?

Levi's message reads: Can you come over? Need to show you something.

I climb out of bed, wincing at my sore hamstrings. A month ago I would've fixed my hair, put on cute underwear and a lacy bra, and slathered lotion on my body. Maybe I would've even worn a little lip gloss. Tonight I pull on his sweatshirt and ripped jeans over my cotton underwear and sports bra.

When I get to his place, I expect to find him out front waiting on me, but he's not there. His mom is on the front porch, though, drinking a glass of red wine while flipping through a file folder. Country music softly pours out of a speaker. Pepper is lying on the stoop secured to her leash. I'm surprised the dog's not with Levi, wherever he is.

"Maggie, hi," Ms. Lucassen says, setting down her glass and standing to give me a hug. "Levi's out back by the lake," she says. Pepper lumbers to her feet and barks and wags her tail, itching to tag along with me.

"No, baby," Ms. Lucassen tells the dog. "You have to stay with me tonight."

Okay, that's weird.

I edge around the side of the house and make my way across the green grass toward the water. I try not to think about the first time we kissed out here. If I had a time machine, I would go back to warn myself not to start something that wouldn't end well. Our kisses—our hookups—they felt like winning races, but they weren't worth almost losing my best friend.

They weren't worth my heart feeling this broken.

I find Levi down by the lake. He's wearing a ball cap turned backward, a gray, long-sleeved tee, athletic shorts, and sneakers. It's warm enough he doesn't need the tights anymore.

"Mags," he calls. "Watch where you step."

Huh?

He points at the sand, where I see tiny shadows shuffling in the moonlight.

Turtles!

"Martha's babies!" I squeal.

They emerge covered with sand, poking up their little heads. They are so tiny! Like the size of a sand dollar. They make their way down to the water, crawling over pebbles.

We watch as they continue to emerge one by one from the sand, entering the great big unknown that will either carry you or let you sink, unless you learn to swim and master it.

"Thanks for inviting me to come watch," I say, and we settle into a nice silence with the brand new turtles. It's funny to imagine one of these little guys becoming a resident terror turtle like Martha one day.

"Maggie," he says quietly, turning toward me. "Can we talk?"

"Of course."

He takes off his cap and drags a hand through his hair. "I realized something in Atlanta."

"Yeah?"

"I wasn't as happy as I thought I'd be after I got my cuts in 100."

"What's wrong?" I rush to say. "You've been working toward this your whole life!" After winning first place at Junior Nationals and qualifying for a second event at the Olympic trials, his name was splashed all over the Tennessee papers, and the major swimming websites mentioned his name as a serious swimmer to watch in the NCAA when he goes to college. Even USA Swimming tweeted about him qualifying in a second event. Everything is coming together for him. Is he starting to feel pressured like Jason?

But what comes out of my best friend's mouth is not about feeling pressured. It's not what I expect at all.

"I miss you."

I touch his arm. "I'm right here, Leaves."

"I made a serious mistake. I shouldn't have tried to push you away… I was scared. I've never had a girlfriend before and wasn't ready to deal with the idea of fitting that into my schedule. But the truth is, I want…I want you more than anything."

I gasp.

"I know I was an ass," he goes on, stepping closer to gently touch the frayed hem of my sweatshirt. My body begins to tremble all over. I can't breathe.

"Do you like Noah?" he asks.

I shrug a little. I do like the idea of going out with a guy and just having fun. Where there's not much risk involved. But is love without risk really love at all? Or is it a shortcut to nowhere?

My heart hurt so much after Levi broke it. To be honest, it's still cracked, and it's been hard work piecing it back together. I'm glad our friendship survived, but I am not sure I want to risk it again.

Plus, I don't have my cuts yet. I need to stay focused. Now

is not the time for more emotional ups and downs. I only have bandwidth to focus on one thing—swimming or this thing with Levi—and right now, swimming comes first.

"I want to see how my date with Noah goes, I guess," I say quietly.

He grasps my hands. "Before the state championship," he starts, "you said we should talk after the race. I wasn't ready then, but I am now."

A tear drips down my cheek. "Levi, I love you."

His eyes flare. "I love you t—"

I interrupt him before I start bawling. "You're my best friend, but what you did to me sucked so much. It was the most important race of my life, and you hurt me so you wouldn't have to deal with your feelings."

"And I told you. I know I was a dick that day. I'm asking for another chance." His eyes are bright blue and shiny like the sparkling stars above.

I stare out at the beach. Another baby turtle pokes his head out of the ground. He emerges from the hole, gangly and dirty with sand. He walks purposefully down to the water, where little waves lap over his shell and clean him up.

I turn and reach for Levi. He swallows me in a hug. His body fits perfectly against mine. It would be so easy to tilt my chin so he can kiss along my jaw. But I'm trembling worse than I did at my driver's test.

I've lost races in my life. Quite a few actually, and every single one hurt. Not one race—not even losing that state championship race to Roxy—hurt as much as Levi deliberately trying to push me away. How bad would it hurt if I let him back in and he left me again?

What happens when we leave for college?

"I need some time to think," I say, pulling away. "And some sleep."

His face is sad as he nods. "I'll pick you up in the morning."

I squeeze his hands. "Good night."

After one last look at the tiny turtles, I head home.

～～

"Maggie! Why don't you own anything cute?"

"They're pajamas," I reply. "Not a prom dress."

Georgia came over to help me plan for my date next weekend, and digging through my pajama drawer frustrates her to no end.

"You need something sexy!"

"No, I don't. These red pajamas are fine."

She gives my plaid pj's a horrified look. "My granddad wears those."

At first I was excited about having a date to the pajama party. Then Levi told me how he feels. Part of me wonders if I should cancel on Noah, but that seems rude. And probably premature, because I have no idea what to do about Levi.

Georgia opens my laptop and types "sexy pajamas" into the search engine. "Oooh, what about this leopard print?"

"Georgia. No."

"C'mon! How about these policewoman pajamas? You can carry handcuffs."

"No! What are you going to wear?" I ask her.

"Hello Kitty."

That gives me an idea. I type into the search box. Pictures pop up and Georgia's eyes balloon. "That's definitely sexy."

I click on the pajamas and order them because they remind me of Levi.

"Are you going with David?"

She nods. "Get this. My mother loves him."

"Really?" That's surprising. Georgia's mom sticks her nose up at pretty much everybody, even the preacher at church.

"I was shocked," Georgia says. "At first it made me wonder whether Hunter is right, that I could do better, because who wants to date a guy their totally strict mother approves of? But then David kissed me, and it was pretty good."

I smile. "So you're sticking with him?"

"For now. We're having fun."

"Is it serious?"

She looks down at her twined fingers. "I don't know. I'm not sure if I'm ready for serious yet. I like what you said about experimenting, because I'm getting used to dating again…and part of me wants to be single when I get to college."

Based on the magazines in Mom's office at King's Royal

Engagements, it seems like society doesn't interpret being single as a positive. We spend a lot of time dressing up, putting on makeup, removing unwanted hair, going on dates, all in the hope of finding someone to spend our lives with.

Before Levi, nothing—not even finding a soul mate—was as important as swimming. Now? I want someone to talk to at night, to tell about how practice went that day. I want to cuddle with a guy who finishes my sentences…and works out the annoying knots in my shoulders.

But it's okay to be single too. I'm glad Georgia's figuring out what she wants, or in this case, simply going with the flow. She's okay with being with a guy who might be great *for now,* but maybe not forever.

The next day at lunch, the sophomore who lives in Levi's neighborhood appears at our table. She scoots a chair between Levi and me. I raise my eyebrows at him, only to find he's focused on her.

"Patches had such a good time playing with Pepper yesterday," she says. "My mom was pissed the dog came home all wet and muddy, but Patches was happy."

Levi grins. "My dog is totally going to corrupt your dog."

"Can they play again soon?"

"I have practice every day this week, but maybe Friday after school? By the way, do you know my friends?" He introduces us all to Rebecca.

She looks at me for a sec, then turns back to Levi. "There's going to be a puppy bowl at the pajama party this year. Do you and Pepper want to come with me and Patches?"

Levi looks at me over Rebecca's shoulder. "If I'm not too tired that night, then sure. Pepper always likes getting out of the house."

My heart deflates. Levi told me he wants another chance, and I said I needed time to consider it. How much time do I get? I hope he's not interested in Rebecca—but even if he isn't, there will eventually be another girl.

It's something I don't want to think about.

The day before the pajama party, I'm lounging on the back deck in my bikini, trying to tan. And by trying to tan, I mean burn. The thing about my skin is it will eventually bronze, but it has to burn a little first. Then I turn from a lobster into a giant freckle.

Tanning is the perfect excuse to relax and figure out my life. Try to, anyway. A flock of geese fly across blue skies in a perfect V. If only my relationship with Levi was that clear.

I love him. I want a relationship with him. But we're going to different colleges, and both of us have full plates. Do we need to add one more stressor? More than anything, I want him to be happy—and for me to be happy too. He said I'm more important to him than swimming. I believe that. And I believe he wants to be with me. A sharp pain fills my chest at the idea of losing him.

Mom pokes her head out the back door. "Tadpole, Hunter's here. He's in the den."

I take off my sunglasses, slip my cover-up over my head, and go inside to find Hunter hunched over on the couch, his eyes puffy and red.

"Are you okay?" I say in a rush.

Looking up at me, he nods slowly. "Can I have something to drink, please?"

In the kitchen I pour him a glass of water, then rejoin him on the couch, where he's staring at the unlit fireplace.

"What's up?"

He takes the water from my hand, drinking most of it in one go. "Shelby ended it with me for good."

"What? I thought you guys were going to stay casual until you leave!"

"We had a big fight about whatever the hell our relationship is. She said things would be different if I were going to college somewhere nearby...so I told her I'd back out of the Air Force Academy if that's what it took." My eyes go wide, and he goes on. "I said I'd go to school in Tennessee. And then she got really mad."

"Why?"

He sets the empty glass on the side table. "She said she wasn't letting me throw away the Air Force for her. I'm going there because every guy in my family went...and I want to serve my country, but I want her too."

Hunter leans over and buries his face in his hands. I rub his shoulder.

"Shelby said we need to end this now before we get in any deeper, and I told her I love her…and then she asked me to leave."

"Oh God," I mumble. "That sucks."

"I know she loves me."

Based on what she said at the baseball game, I think she does too. "Hunter, Shelby really cares about you. That's why she wants you to go to the Air Force Academy. You've been working toward it for so long. You're going to be their star pitcher!"

He smiles a little. His stomach suddenly rumbles.

"Hungry?"

"Not really."

It rumbles again.

"Not hungry, my ass." I fish my cell phone out of the sofa cushions to order takeout. "Pizza?"

Hunter rubs his watery eyes with a thumb and forefinger. "It's Jiffy Burger night."

"We don't have to go. I'll invite everybody over here."

"That sounds good. I don't much feel like going out."

I message Georgia and Levi to get their butts over to my house. We're doing something different for dinner.

Georgia arrives ten minutes later, followed closely by Levi. She sees that Hunter is totally wrecked and sits with him on the couch. Levi joins me on the love seat.

We've talked since he declared his feelings for me but not about anything important—unless you count his story about Pepper escaping her bath at the groomer's, darting through the pet store, and shaking soapy water all over a cage full of angry hamsters.

My nose catches a whiff of Levi's cedar scent, reminding me of the time we got tangled up on these cushions and he worshipped my body.

When Levi sees me looking at him, he clears his throat. "What's going on? Why aren't we going to Jiffy Burger?"

Hunter goes through his story again for Georgia and Levi, and she throws herself at Hunter, hugging him tight.

"I'm here for you," Georgia whispers to him, and he rests his forehead against hers.

Levi and I stare at each other.

I can't imagine life without him. And even though we're going to separate colleges, I would figure out how to make it work. I could do long distance. I'd video chat with him every night. I'd take the risk of not seeing my boyfriend every day for us to be together. I would want him any way I can have him.

But I still don't know whether I could stand the pain of losing him again.

The pizza arrives, and my friends sit in the den to eat. Georgia also raids Dad's party supply closet, finding fake coconut cups with little umbrellas. We drink our water out of them as if we're lounging at the beach together.

It's not Jiffy Burger, but it's still fun. We're still together. And even though we're going to college, maybe things won't automatically change between us.

Maybe sometimes a little change is good.

⌒⌒

I smile at myself in the mirror.

On the night of the pajama party, I put on my pajamas and some light makeup. I even straighten my hair into a long, brown, shiny curtain. It looks good.

When I go downstairs before my first ever date, Mom gives me a hug. "You look so grown-up."

Meanwhile, Dad is horrified. "Go change your clothes right now."

I glance down at my outfit. I'm not even showing cleavage! "Everything is covered up." I pause to take in what Mom and Dad are wearing—matching onesies that make them look like human-sized sock monkeys. "Besides, your outfits are frightening. You will scare little kids."

"That's all part of my plan," Dad says with a laugh.

The doorbell rings. Before the sock monkeys embarrass me, I rush to answer the front door. It's Noah.

He scans my outfit. "Wow, you look great."

I check him out too. He's wearing a dark green bathrobe. Hmm. Very dad-like. Noah's pajamas do not elicit a "wow" from me, that's for sure. But then, Levi could pick me up in the rattiest pajamas ever, and I'd still be beaming.

Noah escorts me out to his car and opens the passenger door for me. I slide inside, wondering if I should be going on a date with a guy I don't have feelings for. I don't want to hurt him. Even if Levi is going with Rebecca and their dogs, it isn't fair to Noah to lead him on. I need to tell him. I don't want to hurt him the way I was hurt before.

Before he starts the engine, I reach over and rest a hand on his forearm. "Noah, I need to tell you something."

He turns to me. "Yeah?"

"Tonight…can we go as friends?"

His eyebrows furrow. "You mean you don't want this to be a date?"

"I was really looking forward to this, but I'm not sure I have romantic feelings for you. I'd rather go as friends."

He lets out a long breath of air. "Sure. Friends. We can do that."

The pajama party is taking place at the Franklin town square, and it spills over onto the fairgrounds. A Ferris wheel circles through the night sky, and the moon bounce looks supremely bouncy.

It's so crowded we have to park on the road about half a mile away and walk up to the party. Our first stop is the fire department, where they have two big engines out front for kids to climb all over and explore. Noah is excited to hop up and pretend to drive the wheel. Meanwhile, I'm excited to check out the firefighters, who do elicit a *wow* from me. And I thought swimmers had muscles.

Once Noah's done on the fire truck, he hops back to the ground in his bathrobe. "Want to go check out the photo booth?"

"Okay."

We chat as we walk over to the photo area. Diane Musgrave set up a studio where people could have their picture taken in front of various world landmarks, like the Pyramids at Giza and the Great Wall of China. Dad did the same thing last year with his Kimono themed party: people could have their picture made with a field of cherry blossoms, Mount Fuji, or Japan's Imperial Palace.

But the line is really long.

"Do you want to do something else?" Noah asks.

"Yes, *please*," I reply, and explain about my dad's rivalry with Musgrave.

"Why doesn't he sue her for copying his ideas?"

"I don't think it works like that."

Noah and I get in line for the bumper cars and then race our little cars around the rink. I discover I'm just as scared of driving these as driving a regular car. Idiots from school keep ramming me head-on, jolting my bones. This better not mess me up for swim practice tomorrow.

When that horror is over, Noah leads me to the dance. Musgrave really missed the mark here. Instead of making this barn look like an elegant ballroom in a German castle or something, she decorated it to look like an Amazon jungle…? Monkey sounds fall from strategically placed speakers.

This will give Dad a coronary.

"Want to dance?" Noah asks.

The last time I slow danced was with Dad at my aunt's wedding a couple years ago, and I stepped all over his feet, so I hope I can manage dancing with a guy. I mean, I swim a flawless backstroke—I should be able to shuffle my feet back and forth. My hands go to Noah's shoulders and he holds my waist. We sway slowly during the song. Being in his arms doesn't feel right though. It's like listening to an off-pitch singer.

If a bad song comes on the radio, you turn it off. What am I doing here?

I want to go find Levi.

"Noah," I start. "I need—"

Before I can get out the rest of my speech, he leans forward and kisses me. I break away. I didn't feel even the slightest spark.

"I'm sorry," I tell him. "I can't."

"Was it that bad?"

"Huh?"

"The kiss?" he mumbles, ruffling and flattening his hair, embarrassed.

"Oh, I liked the kiss. It's just…"

He puts some distance between us. "You love Levi?"

"Is it that obvious?"

"Yeah, I kind of figured." He blows out a heavy breath of air. "But since you're not with him, I thought I'd see if something's there between you and me. You're so nice…"

"I'm sorry if I gave you the wrong impression. I don't really know what I'm doing—I haven't dated anyone before."

"I get what you mean. Sometimes I feel like I'm the only guy who hasn't had a girlfriend," he says quietly.

A few months ago, I thought I was going to be the only college student who'd never had sex or fooled around. But that can't be true. Everyone moves at their own pace when it comes to this stuff. Georgia is taking things slow with David. It took her a couple weeks to share that he'd asked her out. Meanwhile, Hunter wants Shelby on a serious emotional level while she only wants the physical. Noah's a super cute basketball player who hasn't had a girlfriend. And that's fine.

Why was I trying to force myself to move more quickly than was natural?

I guess Levi was right all along. He told me to wait until I found someone I cared about. And it doesn't even have to be someone I love, just someone I feel something for. And as nice as Noah is, I don't feel anything for him. Not like Levi.

I feel a lot for Levi.

Noah looks upset as he pulls his car keys out of his bathrobe pocket, and I feel terrible I hurt him. Maybe it was selfish of me to keep this date.

"Can I take you home?" he asks.

"I think I'll hang out here for a bit."

"Me too."

After a good-bye hug, Noah joins a group of guys from the basketball team who are hanging out with some girls from school. I hope one of them likes him and is deserving. He's a great guy, even if he's not the one for me.

I take off for the catering tent where I know I'll find Mom and Dad. I need to test Diane Musgrave's food they've been talking/complaining about for weeks.

In the tent, I find Levi. I thought he was coming with Rebecca and their dogs. But I only see Levi. Mom the sock monkey is pointing at various hors d'oeuvres, and he's sampling them one by one. Oh. My. God. He's wearing Superman pajamas! His body really fills them out in all the right places. I swallow hard.

I walk over to them as Levi tries a tiny egg roll.

"It all tastes bland to me," he says through a mouthful. "It needs some King's secret sauce."

"Don't let my husband hear you say that," Mom replies. "He'll be drizzling that stuff on everything."

"Hi," I say.

Levi looks up from his egg roll and gapes at my pajamas. He looks me up and down, and starts choking.

Mom slaps his back and asks, "How's your date going, Tadpole?"

"It's over already," I say, and Levi's eyes dart to mine.

"Is everything okay?" Mom rushes to ask.

"It was fine… It just wasn't going to work out." I turn to Levi. "Can I talk to you?"

"Sure." He takes one more egg roll for the road, tossing it in his mouth and brushing off his hands.

Mom's eyebrows pop up as he follows me out of the tent into the warm night.

Once we're under the stars, I loop my arm around his elbow, leading him toward the rides. His warm hand seals comfortably over mine.

"Where're Rebecca and Pepper?"

"I had to let Rebecca down gently… She was getting a bit clingy…and I couldn't think of a bigger disaster than bringing Pepper to town. Remember when I took her to that football game, and she ran onto the field to try and steal the ball? Here, she'd be knocking over toddlers and stealing hot dogs from strangers."

I laugh. "I bet she'd jump in the moon bounce."

"No bet."

"Hey, you want to moon bounce?"

"Of course I want to moon bounce," he replies. "But we need to talk first. What's going on? What happened with Noah?"

We sit down on a bench in front of City Hall as a couple in pajamas with a baby stroller passes by. The bell tower gleams brightly in the moonlight.

"Levi," I start, inhaling sharply, hoping the extra air will fill me with courage. "I like you. I like you so much. And I want something more with you."

His blue eyes capture mine. "Are you sure?"

"Enough to give us a shot."

He leans closer, pressing his forehead to mine. "I want to try too. I've never felt like this before."

I settle my cheek against his. It's smooth and warm, and he smells perfect, like cedar and aftershave. Like *him*. He squeezes my hand.

"I love your pajamas," I whisper in his ear.

"I knew you would." He smirks a little. "I got them for you."

"You did?"

"I kinda had to. I had nothing to wear. I mean, I generally sleep naked." He wiggles his eyebrows and I slap his arm, feeling my face flush red at the thought of him in bed in the buff. He goes on, "I like your pajamas too."

I wore a form-fitting black jumpsuit with little cats on it…and some cat ears on top of my head. Yup, I am Catwoman.

He stretches an arm around the back of our bench, caressing my shoulder. I inch closer to his side. It feels so good to be curled up against him again. His warmth makes me let out a sigh.

Since I started us on this path, I decide to take the next step. Leaning toward him, I press my mouth to his. My fingers draw the letter *M* on his chest, and I hear his sharp intake of breath. We fit perfectly.

He pulls away to look at my face, a lock of his hair falling into his eyes. I push it to the side.

"So are we together now?" he asks.

I keep drawing my initials—*MK MK MK*—all over him with my pointer finger, marking him as mine. "Like you're my boyfriend?"

He answers with another long kiss, his lips devouring me like I'm dessert.

"Will you go to prom with me?" I ask him. "You know, if our race ends in time?"

He takes my hand, brings it to his lips, and kisses two of my knuckles, sending shivers up my spine. "Yes. But only if you dress up as Catwoman again."

I lean against his side, and we watch the people of our small town walk around together, enjoying life, and I smile, knowing ours is only getting started.

Sharks and Minnows

One more chance.

This is my final opportunity to qualify for the Olympic trials.

Sure, I'm sure I'll become a better swimmer in college, and I can try for the trials again in four years. But you only live once, and I am going to give this my all.

Two days before the meet, Coach drives the seven of us in a van to Cincinnati. Only Levi has qualified for Omaha, so technically he doesn't need to race, but he needs the practice and experience in long course. That's part of the reason we're leaving early—to get some practice time in the big pool.

I check Twitter during the ride. Several swimming accounts are saying things like, *Last chance weekend for the #OlympicTrials! If you or your swimmer gets a cut, tweet us!*

Sitting next to me, Levi peeks at my phone, sees what I'm looking at, and whispers in my ear, "Deep breaths."

Coach takes us out for Italian the night before the meet so we can salad and carbo load. At the restaurant, Levi stretches an arm around the back of my chair, keeping me close. We've been seriously dating for about a month now, and everything about it feels right. Part of me wishes we'd started seeing each other years ago, but the other half is glad we waited until we were older and mature enough to handle the responsibility, to ensure our friendship stayed strong.

Susannah is ridiculously excited we're finally together. She keeps squealing and clapping her hands, which is getting on Coach Josh's last nerve. Rolling his eyes, he rips a breadstick in two, demonstrating what he thinks of his swimmers dating. I don't care though. My muscles feel great, I'm eating ravioli, and my boyfriend is rubbing my thigh under the table. It doesn't get much better than this.

Back at the hotel, Coach pulls me aside to sit down on a sofa in the bustling lobby. I figure he's going to give me a lecture about swimcest, but it turns out he wants to discuss the meet.

"Maggie," he says. "We need to talk about tomorrow." Coach claps his hands together, then unclasps them nervously. "Listen, I entered you in the prelims for 400 and 800 freestyle."

"What?" I say. I never swim that far in races. I'm no sprinter, but I wouldn't say I'm a distance specialist either.

So that's why it's surprising when Coach says, "I think you are maturing into a distance specialist."

"What?"

"Your 200 free is getting better and better, especially in long course. I want to stretch it out even more. Let's try it."

"Why'd you wait until now to tell me?"

"You overanalyze things. I wanted to throw you in the pool tomorrow morning and see how it goes. No thinking."

"But won't this wear me out for 200 back and free?"

"Maybe, but I think you'll have a better chance in a longer race than in either of those. So how about it?"

I've been with Coach Josh ten years. I trust him with my life. "All right."

He smiles. "Good. Now off to bed with you." He points over his shoulder at the hotel bar. "I'm gonna try to catch some of the Braves game."

I ride the elevator to my room. When I get there I find Levi sitting on the floor outside the door, one hand buried in his long hair while the other is holding a loved, worn copy of *Harry Potter and the Sorcerer's Stone*.

He started the series over again.

I slide to the carpet beside him, pecking his cheek. He turns his mouth to meet mine and we share sweet, soft kisses.

"What did Coach want?"

I wave a hand. "I'm out of the pool. I don't want to talk swimming tonight. I just want to spend time with you."

"Hot tub, then?" he asks with a tempting smile.

We change into swimsuits and meet Susannah and Jason down at the hotel pool. Swimmers from all over the country are here, and of course they are hogging the hot tub. While Jason starts a noisy cannonball contest, Levi and I stretch out on a lounge chair, curling up under an extra-large beach towel to sneak kisses. We spend a lot of time doing this lately. We love lying on the trampoline in his backyard, kissing through sunsets and cuddling under twinkling stars.

His fingers brush the waistband of my bikini bottoms, making me feel naughty. I'm glad I bought those condoms at the Quick Pick, even if it was the most embarrassing moment in the history of the entire universe.

I lean close to Levi's ear. "You would not believe what happened to me," I say, recounting how I ran into Dad while buying them. I end the tale with, "And then Dad basically said, 'Condoms on me!'"

Levi, of course, dies laughing at my story. I tickle his stomach in retaliation.

"Stop, stop!" he cries, grabbing my hands.

"For a price. One kiss."

He pecks my mouth, and I stop wrestling him, and our touches turn gentle, then more heated. My fingertips draw circles on his chest. He stares into my eyes, a tiny smile on his mouth. Ever since we got together, we've been taking it slow, working our way back to where we were before. Last night we got a bit crazy and went skinny-dipping in Normandy Lake. He made me feel so good, it was probably illegal.

We haven't slept together yet—but I'm ready. I want to show him with my mind and heart and body how much I love him.

"Want to go to your room?" I whisper, my intent clear.

His expression grows heated, full of love and passion, but he shakes his head. "Let's wait until after the meet."

"You're sure?"

Levi cuddles me close. "I'm very happy right now."

"Me too."

At least until Coach Josh shows up on the pool deck and orders us all to bed.

As Susannah and I are getting ready for sleep, putting on pajamas, brushing our teeth, and washing faces, she asks me yet again if I've slept with Levi.

"No."

"Are you going to tell me when you do?"

"No."

"C'mon!" she whines. "I'll tell you when I do it with Jason."

Shocked, I accidentally drop my toothbrush. It clangs into the sink. "You're gonna do it with Jason? That's swimcest!"

She smirks. "Look who's talking."

"Are you guys going to start dating?"

Susannah shrugs. "I'd be into it if he is. He's pretty hot, right?"

"Yup."

"I have an idea! I'll tell him I need to sleep in his room tonight because you and Levi want alone time."

I inhale sharply, loving the idea of spending the night with Levi. But I don't want it to interfere with my race tomorrow. On the other hand, being in his arms helps me sleep better.

"Okay," I say with a smile, as my heart begins to race.

Susannah checks her reflection in the mirror, then opens the hotel room door. "Don't do anything I wouldn't do!"

A minute later, a knock sounds on the door. With a deep breath, I open it to reveal a barefoot Levi in track pants and a soft gray T-shirt.

"Hi."

"Hi," I reply quietly.

"Susannah sent me over. She said something about you wanting to be alone with me?" he flirts.

I give him a teasing smile. "I need another lesson."

"Oh yeah?" He steps into the room, dead bolting the door behind him, and in less time than it takes to swim a fifty-meter sprint, he has our pajamas off and strewn across the carpet. He lays me back on the bed, his hands depressing the pillow on either side of me as he kisses my lips. The minty taste of toothpaste fills my mouth. His weight presses between my legs, and in no time at all he has me panting. Panting, and wanting more.

"Are you sure you don't want to do it tonight?" I whisper.

His eyes meet mine. "I'd love to, but I don't want you to have any regrets tomorrow during the meet. It's too important."

"I won't regret it, I promise, it's just…"

"It's just what?" he asks sweetly.

I weave a hand through his blond hair, taking him all in. "I want it to be good for you."

His eyebrows furrow. "You're worried about that?"

"Yeah, I mean, you've been with other girls."

He kisses me deeply. "You're the best kisser I've ever had. The best hugger. The best hand holder. The best everything. It's because of *you*—because we're right for each other."

I sigh deeply, nuzzling my face in his throat. "So you'll teach me what to do, right?"

"Mags, I think it's gonna be the other way around…"

"I have no idea what I'm doing. What could I possibly teach you?"

"I don't know, but," he takes a deep breath, "you taught me how to love."

I caress up and down his back. "I love you too."

"Do you have those condoms you bought at the store?"

I take a sharp breath. "In my bag."

He finds the protection and brings one to the bed. "I want you to know I'm clean, okay?"

I nod, happy to know it, and glad we're going into this with no secrets. No regrets.

Just love and passion and friendship.

The next morning, I am amped up. My body feels great, and my stress is gone. This meet is mine.

At the pool, "Spring Spotlight" banners hang from the rafters, where clusters of chatting swimmers make predictions for today. Music blares from the speakers. The water is a gleaming pearl blue. The facility smells fresh, and the air feels charged with energy, like right before a lightning storm.

I take deep, steadying breaths in the shower, and out on the pool deck, I make sure to stretch all my limbs really well. Levi even makes time to massage the shoulder that gives me problems, his thumb expertly working that annoying spot. I lean my head back to stare up at him.

"Thank you," I say, and he dips over and kisses me upside down, Spider-Man style. After last night, I feel closer to him than ever before, and I love that my best friend was my first. It wasn't flawless—it took us a bit to find the right angle and our rhythm, but in the end it was perfect.

I run into Roxy at the practice lanes. "Good luck!" I call to her. She gives me a head nod but otherwise ignores me. And I'm happy with that. I won't bother her, and she won't bother me. Today is between me and the water.

The prelims for 200 free and back go okay. I get placed in the A final for 200 free and B final for 200 back, which kind of sucks. I always thought 200 back was my best event, but maybe Coach is right. Maybe I'm evolving. Not that I won't continue to swim my butt off in that race, but I'm open to new options. Like 400 free. For an event I've never done in long course, I do great in the prelims thanks to my endurance and get put into the A final. To qualify for the trials, I need a 4:17.99.

While waiting on the finals later in the day, Levi and I hover near the pool with Jason and Susannah, cheering on our teammates. Levi stands right behind me, pressing his chest to my back, kissing the top of my head.

"I was thinking," he whispers in my ear. "Later we should play sharks and minnows. I'll be the minnow this time, and you'll be the big, mean shark that comes after me. And when you catch me, you can—"

"Maggie, you're on!" Coach calls. It's time to warm up for the 400 free final. Levi gives me a good luck hug.

After a few laps in the warm up pool, I step up to the blocks, adjusting the straps of my suit and tightening my goggles one last time. I shake my arms out and slap my muscles. The announcer says, "On your mark."

One last deep breath.

The buzzer sounds and I fly off the blocks.

People are cheering as I pull myself along on top of the water. Out of the corner of my eye, I see other swimmers accelerating. But Coach's voice is clear in my mind: *you'll catch them on the back end.* Stay steady. In the second half of the race, I go after it, working to close the gap. I focus on keeping my elbows high to maintain a smooth, steady stroke. Kick, kick, kick. On the final fifty, I try to improve a little, kicking harder with my legs while keeping the same tempo with my arms. I twirl around to face the scoreboard. Third place! My time is 4:15.89! Two seconds faster than I needed!

"Oh my God!" I scream, slapping the water. I did it!

It was such a fast heat two other girls also get Olympic trial cuts. The announcer shouts over the loudspeaker that we're going to Omaha. Tears roll down my cheeks. All my hard work, years upon years in the pool, led to me having awesome endurance. It led me to this moment.

In June, I will be going to the biggest meet of my life!

Coach Josh gives me a big hug, and then I rush for my boyfriend. He lifts me up into his arms, spins me in a circle (which is probably an unsanctioned activity), and kisses me in front of a cheering crowd. Everything is great until Jason runs up and smacks me on the butt with a kickboard.

When I call Mom and Dad, they scream congratulations over and over, which is pretty funny considering they are catering a library fund-raiser tonight. It's fun to imagine the librarians shushing them.

Then Levi and I sit in the stands to watch the rest of the finals and cheer for New Wave. My heart won't stop racing. My smile feels permanently glued to my face. I can't sit still. I did it!

Levi peeks at the time on his phone. It's 6:30 p.m. "Looks like we won't make it back in time for prom."

I lean against his side, resting my cheek against his shoulder. "That's okay. This is better than some dance."

"You're damn right it is," he says. "But I still want you to have your prom."

He tugs me up out of my seat, leads me into the hallway, and disappears into the guys' locker room. He comes out a moment later with a small cooler and a shopping bag. From it he pulls a wireless speaker, which, after a flick of his thumb on his phone, begins to play a slow classical song. He also fishes out a candle, lights it, and places it on the ground. The cooler reveals a plastic box containing a white orchid corsage decorated with bright blue pearls. This he gently slips onto my wrist.

"I love it," I tell him, and he steals a quick kiss. Still in our suits and sweats, he pulls me into his arms and starts slow dancing with me.

Everything is perfect.

I'm with my best friend.

Four Years Later...

A Sam Henry Epilogue for Hundred Oaks Fans

Must. Stay. Awake.

Must. Stay. Awake.

In the past when I saw new parents, I never understood why they were so exhausted all the time. Then I became a dad and learned babies must be fed constantly. That's all my baby does. Eat. Which isn't surprising considering how much his mom and I love food.

I stare down at my beautiful son as I balance his tiny body on my thighs. I run my fingers over his wisps of light hair. *Just like Mom and Dad.*

"Sean's going to be a great wide receiver one day," I say.

Jordan gives me a look of horror. "He's a quarterback!"

"Wide receiver."

She lifts one of Sean's tiny arms between her thumb and forefinger. "Look at these guns. He's a born quarterback."

"He can pick whatever position he wants," I say, leaning down to kiss his forehead.

Jordan yawns. "With our luck, he'll end up hating football and want to play chess or something."

"He'd be the best chess player in the world."

At my words, Jordan snuggles closer to me.

We're sitting on the couch in the den of the new house we bought a few months ago. It's only seven o'clock in the evening, but our eyelids are drooping, and we can't stop yawning no matter how much coffee we drink. Of course the baby is wide awake because he's a Henry, and Henrys are born troublemakers. Instead of sleeping, Sean is busy making gurgling noises and looking around. I have no idea what he's looking at though. They say babies can't see very far away when they're first born, and he's only a week old.

A week old, and already the most popular guy in Franklin. Pretty much every person we know has dropped by to see him. My sister, Maya, and her fiancé, Jesse, love Sean so much they've been here every day. In addition to a little Braves onesie, they brought him an acoustic guitar. What is he supposed to do with it? I mean, I know he's my son and he's going to be great at everything, but he can't hold up his head yet, much less a guitar. Still, it's good to know we have built-in babysitters whenever we need them.

And before she got pregnant, Jordan had been training for an eventual triathlon with our friend Matt Brown. Of course he showed up to see the baby, and then immediately asked when Jordan's going to start biking and swimming again. Seeing as how she can't keep her eyes open, I think it might be a little while before she's back at it.

This past week has been all about concentrating on Sean, but now we need to concentrate on something else: staying awake to watch the swimming Olympic trials. Jordan's former students, Maggie and Levi, are both competing for spots on the US Olympic team.

They didn't make the cut four years ago, but there's a good chance they will this time. Levi recently won NCAA Swimmer of the Year, and Maggie led Cal-Berkeley to an undefeated season.

ESPN shows video of Maggie and Levi standing together on the pool deck, laughing at something together. Levi wraps an arm around her waist and kisses her forehead.

The TV announcer says, "Maggie King and Levi Lucassen, both expected to score spots on the US Olympic team, have been dating since high school…"

"Jordan!" I say, not taking my eyes off the screen. I pat her leg. "Woods! They're on! Jordan!"

That's when I hear the snore.

I peek over at Jordan. Her eyes are shut, her mouth wide open.

I've known my wife—my best friend—since we were seven years old. As kids, we would nap together, sleeping head to toe. That's how I know she's always been a snorer. But I will never get tired of it.

I love her.

I pick up the remote to press record so we can watch the trials later.

For now, I'm content to watch her and our son sleep.

Acknowledgments

I had a tough time in high school when it came to relationships. It felt like everyone but me had a boyfriend. Guys hardly ever asked me out. What was I doing wrong? I wore the clothes other girls wore. I did my hair like them too. When I pursued guys who didn't want me as much as I wanted them, it always ended poorly.

As I grew older I began to understand that healthy relationships and physical experiences happen in their own time. Like Maggie, I learned that just because other girls had more physical experience with boys didn't mean I was somehow lacking. I learned I needed to understand who I was as a person, and be myself, before I could be in a relationship with someone else. It was then that I started meeting nice guys who were respectful and funny. If you worry that you won't meet the right person, be kind to yourself and be patient, and everything will be fine.

I love swimming. As a kid, I spent countless hours at the city pool and lake. I know quite a bit about swimming, but not nearly enough to write Maggie and Levi's story! I had a lot of help.

A huge thanks to Evan Stiles and the Arlington Aquatic Club in Arlington, Virginia, for letting me watch your practices and answering a billion questions. I'm grateful for the information online at SwimSwam and USA Swimming. To my first readers, thank you for all your great feedback: Willa Smith, Christy Maier, Andrea Soule, Trish Doller, Ginger Phillips, Rehka Radhakrishnan, and Jen Fisher. Thanks to my editor, Annette Pollert-Morgan, and everyone at Sourcebooks. Thank you to my husband, Don, for his unwavering support. Finally, I'm so appreciative of my readers. I love receiving your emails, tweets, and messages on Facebook, Instagram, and Goodreads. You are the best.

About the Author

Miranda Kenneally grew up in Manchester, Tennessee, a quaint little town where nothing cool ever happened until after she left. Now, Manchester is the home of Bonnaroo. Growing up, Miranda wanted to become an author, a major league baseball player, a country music singer, or an interpreter for the United Nations. Instead, she became an author who also works for the US Department of State in Washington, DC, and once acted as George W. Bush's armrest during a meeting. She enjoys reading and writing young adult literature and loves *Star Trek*, music, sports, Mexican food, Twitter, and coffee. She lives in Arlington, Virginia, with her husband, Don, and cat, Brady. Visit www.mirandakenneally.com.